Sixth Cabin

by

Kathi Daley

D1739238

I want to thank the very talented Jessica Fischer for the cover art.

I so appreciate Bruce Curran, who is always ready and willing to answer my cyber questions; Jayme Maness for helping out with the book clubs; and Peggy Hyndman for helping sleuth out those pesky typos.

And, of course, thanks to the readers and bloggers in my life, who make doing what I do possible.

Thank you to Randy Ladenheim-Gil for the editing.

And finally, I want to thank my husband Ken for allowing me time to write by taking care of everything else.

The Writers' Retreat Residents

Jillian (Jill) Hanford

Jillian is a dark-haired, dark-eyed, never-married newspaper reporter who moved to Gull Island after her much-older brother, Garrett Hanford, had a stroke and was no longer able to run the resort he'd inherited. Jillian had suffered a personal setback and needed a change in lifestyle, so she decided to run the resort as a writers' retreat while she waited for an opportunity to work her way back into her old life. Since then, she has found a home on Gull Island and has decided to stay and work with Jack running the local newspaper.

Jackson (Jack) Jones

Jack is a dark-haired, blue-eyed, never-married, nationally acclaimed author of hard-core mysteries and thrillers, who is as famous for his good looks and boyish charm as he is for the stories he pens. Despite his success as a novelist, he'd always dreamed of writing for a newspaper, so he gave up his penthouse apartment and bought the failing *Gull Island News*.

George Baxter

George is a writer of traditional whodunit mysteries. He'd been a friend of Garrett Hanford's since they were boys and spent many winters at the resort penning his novels. When he heard the oceanfront resort was going to be used as a writers' retreat, he was one of the first to get on board. George is a distinguished-looking man with gray hair, dark green eyes, and a certain sense of old-fashioned style that many admire.

Clara Kline

Clara is a self-proclaimed psychic who writes fantasy and paranormal mysteries. She wears her long gray hair in a practical braid and favors long, peasant-type skirts and blouses. Clara decided to move to the retreat after she had a vision that she would find her soul mate living within its walls. So far, the only soul mate she has stumbled on to is a cat named Agatha, but it does seem that romance is in the air, so she may yet find the man she has envisioned.

Alex Cole

Alex is a fun and flirty millennial who made his first million writing science fiction when he was just twenty-two. He's the lighthearted jokester of the group who uses his blond-haired, blue-eyed good looks to participate in serial dating. He has the means to live anywhere, but the thought of a writers' retreat seemed quaint and retro, so he decided to expand his base of experience and moved in.

Brit Baxter

Brit is George Baxter's niece. A petite blond pixie and MIT graduate, she decided to make the trip east with her uncle after quitting her job to pursue her dream of writing. Her real strength is in social networking and understanding the dynamics behind the information individuals choose to share on the internet.

Victoria Vance

Victoria is a romance author who lives the life she writes about in her steamy novels. She travels the world and does what she wants to who she wants without ever making an emotional connection. Her raven-black hair accentuates her pale skin and bright green eyes. She's the woman every man fantasizes about but none can conquer. When she isn't traveling the world, she's Jillian's best friend, which is why when Jillian needed her, she gave up her penthouse apartment overlooking Central Park to move into the dilapidated island retreat.

Nicole Carrington

Nicole is a tall and thin true crime author with long dark hair, a pale complexion, and huge brown eyes. She has lived a tragic life and tends to keep to herself, which can make her seem standoffish. Initially, she didn't seem to want to be approached for any reason. It didn't seem she would fit in, but she has shown signs of softening up a bit now that she's gotten to know everyone and has even agreed to attend a few of the group dinners the writers share from time to time.

Garrett Hanford

Garrett isn't a writer, but he owns the resort and is becoming one of the gang. He had a stroke that ended his ability to run the resort as a family vacation spot.

He has lived on Gull Island his entire life and has a lot to offer the Mystery Mastermind Group.

Townsfolk

Deputy Rick Savage

Rick is not only the island's main source of law enforcement, he's a volunteer force unto himself. He cares about the island and its inhabitants and is willing to do what needs to be done to protect that which he loves. He's a single man in his thirties who seldom has time to date despite his devilish good looks, which most believe could land him any woman he wants.

Mayor Betty Sue Bell

Betty Sue is a homegrown Southern lady who owns a beauty parlor called Betty Boop's Beauty Salon. She can be flirty and sassy, but when her town or its citizens are in trouble, she turns into a barracuda. She has a Southern flare that will leave you laughing, but when there's a battle to fight, she's the one you most want in your corner.

Gertie Newsome

Gertie is the owner of Gertie's on the Wharf. Southern born and bred, she believes in the magic of the South and the passion of its people. She shares her home with a ghost named Mortie who has been a regular part of her life for over thirty years. She's friendly, gregarious, and outspoken, unafraid to take on anyone or anything she needs to protect those she loves.

Meg Collins

Meg is a volunteer at the island museum and the organizer of the turtle rescue squad. Some feel the island and its wildlife are her life, but Meg has a soft spot for island residents like Jill and the writers who live with her.

Barbara Jean Freeman

Barbara is an outspoken woman with a tendency toward big hair and loud colors. She's a friendly sort with a propensity toward gossip who owns a bike shop in town.

Brooke Johnson

Brooke is a teacher and mother who works hard in her spare time as volunteer coordinator for the community. She met Jack and Jill when she was a suspect in the first case they tackled.

Sully

Sully is a popular islander who owns the local bar and offers lots of information about the goings-on in the community. When Blackbeard manages to escape for a day on the town, one of the first stops he always makes is to see his buddy Sully.

Quinten Davenport

Quinten is a retired Los Angeles County Medical Examiner who is currently dating Gertie. Although retired, Quinten is more than happy to help the Mystery Mastermind Group when they need a medical opinion, and his presence provides stability to   them.

The Victim

Emily Halliwell

Emily is the sixteen-year-old half sister of Writers' Retreat resident Nicole Carrington. She lived with her parents in Bangor, Maine, until the previous March, when she called Nicole to tell her that her father had been abusing her, so she was running away with Slayer, who she'd met in a bar. Nicole expressed her concern for her safety, so Emily promised to send her a selfie every week so she would know she was alive and well. She did until May 15. Nicole hasn't heard from her since the last photo sent, on May 8.

The Other Players

Slayer

A twenty-two-year-old guitar player and drifter met Emily in a bar about a month before they decided to take off on a grand adventure. Nicole doesn't know his current whereabouts or even if he is still with Emily. The photos Emily sent were of her and her alone.

Grunge

Slayer's friend and the drummer for the band he was a part of until he took off with Emily.

Wayne Dillard

A drifter wanted for questioning in the death of a woman in Fort Collins, Maine.

Officer Grant

Police officer in Fort Collins.

Chapter 1

Monday, January 29

Most every Monday evening, the group of writers who live and write at the Gull Island Writers' Retreat meet in the main house, where I, Jillian Hanford, live with my brother, resort owner Garrett Hanford, and paranormal writer Clara Kline. The other writers, who live in cabins scattered around the oceanfront property, gather, not only to socialize but to discuss whichever mystery the Mastermind Group is currently investigating. This week, one of our newer residents, Nicole Carrington, had asked to present a mystery to us. Nicole had moved to the resort two months before in the hope of picking up the trail of her half sister, Emily Halliwell, who ran away from home when she was just sixteen but agreed to maintain contact with her sister via a weekly photo. The last photo Nicole had received arrived on May 8.

"Okay, everyone, let's get right to it," I said once the meal I'd served had been eaten and we'd gathered in a large circle near the stone fireplace to discuss this week's case. "As I've already mentioned, Nicole has a mystery she'd like to present to the group. I thought it best if we gave her the floor so she can lay the groundwork. Feel free to ask any questions you have."

In the two months Nicole had been living at the resort, she'd made it clear to us that she wasn't interested in socializing or engaging in any shared investigations. The fact that she was here tonight had a lot of us feeling uncertain, some of us suspicious.

"Thank you for agreeing to hear my case." Nicole, a tall woman with a thin frame dressed in black dress slacks and a white button-down blouse, smiled weakly. Her pale complexion set off her black hair and huge brown eyes, which had taken on a serious expression when she took the floor. "As I've already explained to Jill, the reason I came to the island wasn't, as I told everyone, to do research for a novel, but to research a missing person. Her name is Emily. She's my half sister and I haven't heard from her since May."

No one spoke, but I could see Nicole had everyone's attention. The group was made up of wonderful people, but Nicole had gone to such lengths to push us away that I wasn't sure how she would be received. Still, I hoped they would find it in their hearts to forgive Nicole and rise to the challenge of locating a teen who could very well need our help.

Nicole made eye contact with each person in the room as she continued. "Emily and I aren't close. She's the product of my mother's second marriage, to a man I've only met once. My mother is a troubled woman. I've only spoken to her a handful of times since I was put into foster care when I was twelve." She paused and took a breath. I couldn't imagine how hard this must be for her. "When Emily was born I was fifteen and living with my third foster family. I was taken from my mother when it became apparent she didn't have what it took to care for or supervise me. I was told that once she completed a series of tasks determined by the court, I'd be returned to her." Nicole cleared her throat, then took a sip of water from the glass on the table near her. "In the beginning, I believed she would fight for me, so I hoped and waited. But as the days turned to weeks, and the weeks turned to months, I began to fear she had moved on without me. When Emily was born, it finally sank in that the person I'd depended on more than anyone in the world was too busy marrying another man and having another baby to even remember the child she'd left behind."

I put a hand to my heart. It was obvious Nicole was still angry about the situation. Not that I blamed her. She appeared to be a very private person and I was willing to bet it had taken her a lot of courage to admit to her feelings of betrayal and, I was sure, inadequacy.

Nicole continued. "After I reached my eighteenth birthday and was free to make my own choices, I got a job, worked hard, and cut my mother out of my life completely. I figured if she didn't have time for me, I didn't have time for her. I didn't see or hear from her or my sister for almost nine years. I saw Emily for the first time at my grandmother's when she was twelve. After I spoke to her, I realized I'd had the better childhood. I won't say we became great friends, but we did begin to text each other from time to time, and I made a point of sending her a gift on her birthday and for Christmas."

Nicole cleared her throat and looked nervously around the room before she continued. "Emily called me on the night she left home. She told me that her father had been beating her and she was done. I didn't blame her for wanting out and offered to let her stay with me. I even offered to drive to Bangor, where she lived with our mother and her father, and pick her up. She said she was grateful for the offer, but she'd met a boy and was in love. She wanted to start a life with this guy, who I know only as Slayer."

I cringed. The name Slayer didn't suggest a guy who would act responsibly and take care of Emily.

Nicole resumed her story. "Emily knew I was worried about her being on her own, so she agreed to send me a selfie once a week to prove she was safe and happy. And she did. Every Monday, up until May 15."

"There was no photo on May 15?" Jackson Jones, a nationally acclaimed author, local newspaper owner, and my boyfriend, asked.

"There was no photo on May 15 or ever again," Nicole confirmed. "The last photo I received was sent on May 8. It took me months to figure out where the last photo was taken, but after more than four months of searching for Emily, following every lead I could carve out of the few clues I had, I determined it was taken right here on Gull Island. Right here at this resort."

"And you had no idea at all where she might have gone after she left here?" Clara, a self-proclaimed psychic and the author of paranormal mysteries, asked.

Nicole shook her head. "None. When she missed sending me a photo for the second week in a row, I grew worried."

"Did you call the police?" Alex Cole, a fun and flirty millennial and nationally best-selling author, asked.

Nicole nodded. "When I hadn't heard from her for three weeks, I called the police in Maine and tried to report her as a missing person. Of course, the first question I was asked was when I had last seen Emily. I had to say it had been over a year since I'd seen her, and I tried to explain about the photos. Finally, I managed to get someone to at least go to speak to Emily's parents. Our mother assured the police that Emily wasn't missing; she'd run away. She painted a picture of a troubled girl who was in to drugs and other illegal activities who had abandoned her loving and dedicated parents despite their effort to get help for her. The officer who spoke to my mother and her pond scum of a husband did file a report, but Emily was listed as a runaway, not as a missing person. I'm pretty sure no one took the time to look for her."

Alex leaned forward, resting his forearms on his thighs and letting his hands hang between them. "You said you hadn't seen Emily in over a year and you weren't really close to her. You also said at the beginning that Emily had run away, so the way police classified her disappearance from her family home was accurate. Are you certain Emily didn't just get tired of sending you photos as she made a life with this guy of hers?"

"No," Nicole admitted. "I'm not certain Emily is in trouble. She may very well have just grown tired of placating me and stopped bothering with the photos. I've tried texting the phone she sent me the photos from hundreds of times, but they remain undelivered. It's possible she lost or damaged the phone, which might also explain why the photos stopped so abruptly. But I need to know that she's okay." Nicole looked Alex in the eye. "If she were your sister, what would you do?"

Alex sat back in his chair, using one hand to swipe his longish hair back from over his eyes. "I guess, like you, I'd need to know for certain. Which leads to my next question. You've been here for months; why didn't you ask for our help before now?"

"Honestly," Nicole looked around the room, "I didn't trust you. Any of you. The last place my sister was seen was here, and then she disappeared. After I got to know everyone, I could see none of you were responsible for her disappearance. I've exhausted every lead, which were slim to begin with. I need your help."

Alex smiled a crooked little smile. "Okay. That's good enough for me."

"You said you've exhausted every clue," George Baxter, a seasoned author of traditional whodunits, began. "Exactly what clues have you found to this point?"

"Not a lot, I'm afraid, but I have a general feel for the route Emily took. I went back through the photos and tried to figure out where they were taken. It wasn't easy because they all had nondescript scenery in the background, but I caught a break and found one of the places she stayed. She had moved on by the time I arrived, of course, but I was able to trace the route she and her boyfriend took to the location of the next photo. Based on things she said to people I spoke to, I could move from the location of one photo to the next. I continued to follow them until I arrived on Gull Island."

"Do you have a copy of the last photo Emily sent?" Jack asked.

Nicole held up a photo she'd had enlarged for the meeting. It featured a smiling young girl with long dark hair and shining blue eyes. She was standing in front of a wooden door with the number six on it.

"*Save the girl, save the girl*," said Blackbeard, Garrett's talkative parrot.

Garrett chuckled. "Yes, that does seem to be the point of this discussion, and yes, the cabin in the photo is one of ours before we remodeled."

Nicole looked directly at Garrett, who was sitting in his wheelchair next to Clara. "The reason I wanted to rent a cabin here in the first place was because my sister's trail died here. When I first contacted Jill, I hoped you would recognize Emily, but then I learned you'd already suffered a stroke and were in the hospital this past May."

"Yes. I'm sorry," Garrett said with sympathy. "The resort was closed after my stroke in late April, until a friend arrived to open it up in June."

"I've since learned that, which is why I'm here this evening. I need your help." Nicole looked around the room. "All of your help. I don't know where Emily is. I don't know if she's dead or alive. What I do know is that this resort is the last place she took a selfie. It's the last place I know she was."

The room fell into silence as everyone processed Nicole's words.

"This is going to be a difficult case," Jack said. "We'll need to ask tough questions. I suspect your instinct might be to protect your sister from information you think she might not want shared, but even small details could be important."

Nicole nodded. "I understand. I'm prepared to be transparent. I just want to find Emily and take her home." Nicole swiped angrily at a tear that slipped down her cheek.

I stood up to divert the group's attention to give Nicole a chance to compose herself. From what I knew about her, she wasn't comfortable with public displays of emotion. "Let's come up with a plan. A place to start. We all have our specialties; let's come up with a plan to use them."

Brit Baxter, a novice blond-haired writer of chick lit and George's niece, began. "I can check the usual social media sites to see if photos or mentions of Emily pop up. I can run a Google search for general information, and if you have a list of the places she visited prior to her arrival here, I can research them as well."

"And I'll consult my cards," Clara offered. She looked at Nicole. "Do you have something personal of hers? Perhaps a hairbrush?"

Nicole looked like she might refuse but then changed her mind and agreed to get something to Clara right away. It seemed obvious to me that Nicole would depend on logic over feelings and clairvoyance, but she also was determined to do whatever was asked of her.

"Alex and I can work together to dig into the backgrounds of both Emily and this Slayer," George volunteered. He glanced at Alex, who nodded.

"I'll pull up as much as I can from news articles that may tie in," Jack spoke up. "And Jill and I will also sit down with Nicole and work up a detailed timeline. Once we have that, it may be necessary for someone to go back and reinterview anyone Nicole has already spoken to."

"I have time and am happy to travel if need be," I offered.

"I'll show Emily's photo to others on the island," Garrett volunteered. "I know a lot of people. Someone must have seen her."

"I'll take you," Clara offered. "I can drive."

I couldn't help but notice the way Garrett smiled at Clara. It almost seemed as if something was going on between them, but I had no proof of anything more than friendship, and it wasn't my business.

I was about to ask Nicole if she had anything she wanted to add when my best friend, romance writer Victoria Vance, walked into the house with our temporary resident, Abby Boston, and her nieces and nephews.

"Sorry to interrupt," Vikki said. "Abby has been released from the hospital and I want to get her settled." Vikki had offered to help with the kids when it became apparent the very pregnant Abby was going to need it. Lord knew she'd had a tough time of it. First, Abby's sister had died, leaving her with her four children to raise, and then Abby's husband had been murdered. To top it all off, shortly before her husband's death, Abby had found out she had a child of her own on the way. When Abby ended up in the hospital with complications, we'd decided she and the kids should stay with us until after the baby was born.

"I'm glad you're home." I smiled at Abby.

She smiled shyly in return.

"I'll help you get everyone settled." Brit popped up. She turned to Nicole. "Don't worry. We'll find your sister."

Nicole sent Brit a look of thanks, then turned back to the rest of the group. "Thank you all for agreeing to do what you can. It means more to me than I can say. I've never had anyone I could depend on. You all are so very lucky to have one another."

******

After everyone returned to their own cabins or rooms, Jack and I took our golden retriever, Kizmet— Kizzy for short—out for a walk. Kizzy had stayed with me while Jack's mother had been visiting him, but now that she'd gone, Kizzy was going to go back to living with him. I was really going to miss her. I'd never wanted a dog before, but now that I'd spent time with one, I realized how the furry little creatures could burrow into your heart, filling in all the dark and empty spaces.

"I spoke to Nicole before she left," I said as we walked hand in hand along the beach. "She agreed to meet with us at nine o'clock tomorrow morning. She'll be ready with copies of maps, photos, and notes to share."

"This isn't going to be easy," Jack cautioned as the waves from the calm sea lapped up onto the shore.

"I know. I think she realizes that too. But God, Jack. A sixteen-year-old girl out on her own with some random guy who might not be trustworthy. We have to try."

Jack squeezed my hand. "And we will. If she can be found, we'll find her."

"You think she's dead," I said in a flat tone.

Jack stopped walking and looked at me. "I think she's either dead or for some reason doesn't want to be found. I can't think of any other reason she'd stop sending the photos all of a sudden the way she did."

Kizzy brought me a stick. I picked it up and tossed it. "She could have been in an accident. She could have amnesia."

Jack put his arm around my shoulders and began walking again. "Yes, there is that. Or she could have been kidnapped. If she's being held captive, we may be able to find the clues we need to track her down."

I laid my head on Jack's shoulder. "I know the odds are that if we solve the mystery, we'll do it by finding something tragic. I hope with my whole heart that isn't true, but it seems to me if someone close to me was missing, I'd want to know. One way or the other, I'd want to know."

Jack kissed the side of my face. "Yeah. Me too."

We continued to walk in silence, each lost in our own thoughts. After a while, Jack spoke. "You said tonight that if it was determined that reinterviewing people Nicole had already spoken to as she traveled south was necessary, you'd do it."

I nodded. "Garrett is doing better, and Clara helps him out with whatever he needs anyway. Brit and Vikki seem to have taken over as caregivers for Abby and the kids, and I know Alex has a deadline he's been struggling with. I suppose George might have time to take a road trip, but I'd worry about him going on his own. He's not exactly a spring chicken. I'm between projects right now, I have interview skills from my days as a reporter, and I want to help. I think it should be me."

"I agree. What I was going to say is that if you go, I'm going with you."

"But you have the paper."

"I can do what I need to do from the road once I get the paper out on Wednesday with the help of my part-timers. I know you're a capable adult and I'm not trying to smother you, but I'd feel more comfortable if I went with you."

I looked at the feisty puppy that was sitting at our feet, waiting for one of us to bend down and pick up the stick. "What about Kizzy?"

"We'll bring her."

I bent down, picked up the stick, and tossed it. "Okay. If, after speaking to Nicole, we feel there would be benefit in reinterviewing the people she's already spoken to, we'll all go. You, me, and the dog."

Chapter 2

Tuesday, January 30

I woke the next morning to an overcast and dreary day. It felt like the perfect sort of day to roll over and go back to sleep, but I had a ton of things to accomplish, and Jack and I were supposed to meet with Nicole at nine. I closed my eyes for a few brief seconds, let out a groan, and slipped out of the warm bed into the chilly room at the top of the house, which I'd claimed as my own. Pulling on fuzzy slippers and a thick sweatshirt, I headed down the stairs, where someone, probably George, had started a fire in both the living room fireplace and the one that served the kitchen and dining area.

"You're all up early," I said to the group gathered around the dining table, which included Brit, Vikki, Garrett, George, Clara, and all four of Abby's children.

"George was kind enough to come over early to start the fires," Vikki explained. "And Brit is going to drive the girls to school after breakfast."

"How's Abby this morning?" I asked.

"Still sleeping, and she was sleeping soundly every time I looked in on her last night." Vikki had temporarily moved back into the main house to keep an eye on Abby and the kids. "I'm going to put cartoons on for the boys after their sisters leave for school. I'll take care of anything Abby needs then. Garrett and Clara have offered to keep an eye on the boys for a few hours this morning while I take care of some work I have. After that, I'll be free to assume the role of Auntie Vikki."

"Based on the huge grin on your face, I assume you're enjoying being an honorary auntie?"

"Very much."

"I think I'll help the boys make cookies later," Clara offered.

"They're three," I reminded her.

Clara shrugged. "Maybe, but I always need tasters, and that's something you can do at any age. Are you going into the newspaper today?"

"Maybe later. Jack and I are meeting Nicole to go over her notes, and to ask any additional questions we come up with."

Brit buttered a piece of toast, took a bite, and then placed the rest on her plate. "I did a quick search of popular social media sites and didn't find anything for a sixteen-year-old Emily Halliwell from Maine. I find that odd. Social media is a huge part of most teenage girls' lives. I'll keep looking, but I suspect she didn't want her parents snooping into her business, so she used some other name for her social media accounts."

"I guess that makes sense," I said. "It does sound as if she didn't have the best relationship with her parents. I can see why she'd use an assumed name to communicate with her friends."

"A lot of teens use aliases," Brit informed me. "Even kids who come from fairly comfortable family situations. Some social media sites are stricter than others about providing legal names and addresses. I'll keep looking."

I looked at Clara. "Did Nicole ever get you a personal item of Emily's?"

"Not yet. I reminded her about it as she was leaving last night. She hadn't seen her sister for quite a while, so she didn't have anything like a hairbrush or a piece of clothing. She asked if something that belonged to her but had been sent by her sister would work. The further removed an object is from whoever I'm seeking, the less likely I am to get a vision, but I'll take whatever she can find and give it a try."

"Do you always need an object to get a reading?" I asked.

"No, not always. But it helps. No matter what, I'll do what I can."

"After we're released from babysitting duties for the day, Clara and I are going into town to show Emily's photo around," Garrett said.

"That's great. I appreciate your help. Both of you."

After everyone had eaten and Brit had left to take Rebecca and Rachael to school, I went upstairs to shower and dress. Jack was meeting me here at about eight-fifty, and then we planned to walk through the resort to Nicole's cabin. She adored Kizzy, so I told Jack to bring her along.

I dressed in a pair of jeans tucked into leather boots, a warm sweater, and a leather jacket to ward off the dampness of the dreary day. Jack arrived right on time, and we let Vikki know what we were doing, then set off down the path that wound through the cabins toward the new cabin six, where Nicole lived. As we passed the path that veered off to the turtle beach where Jack was building his cabin, I asked about his progress. I couldn't wait until the cabin was ready and he and Kizzy became my neighbors.

"The plans and permits are in order. I should be ready to break ground in a few weeks. I have a contractor who's prepared to give me his full attention, so I'm hoping to have the exterior walls up before the turtles come to nest. No matter what, I'm going to take a break during nesting season so I won't disturb them."

"That's really conscientious of you. I'm sure the turtles will appreciate your effort, and I know the turtle squad will as well."

Jack turned and looked at me. "Speaking of the rescue squad, it occurred to me that the turtles would have been nesting when Emily was here in May, which means Digger and the others would have spent time on the beach at the south end of the resort every day. I wonder if any of them might have seen Emily if she was squatting here."

"I don't know, but it would be worthwhile to ask them, or maybe we can suggest to Garrett that he speak to members of the team while he's in town. I'll talk to him when we're done here."

Nicole opened her door before we even had a chance to knock. "Please come in. I have coffee, if you'd like."

Jack and I both said we'd love a cup. Nicole had a chew toy for Kizzy to play with, and I saw she'd laid a furry blanket on the floor for her as well. When I'd first met Nicole, I thought her incapable of demonstrating warmth, but it seemed that since Kizzy had come into the picture, she'd thawed considerably.

"I have everything I've gathered so far on the table." Nicole motioned to a stack of notepads, photos, maps, and manila envelopes. "I'm not sure where to start."

We sat down opposite Nicole, and Jack suggested, "Let's start at the beginning. What can you tell us about Emily before she ran away?"

Nicole began doodling on one of her notepads absentmindedly. "I'm not sure I can tell you much. My mother met and married a man named Dover Halliwell after I was in foster care, and they had Emily shortly afterward. At first, she and Dover lived in Portland, but they moved to Bangor when Emily was five or six. I didn't stay in touch with my mother after I left the foster-care system when I turned eighteen. When I met Emily at my grandmother's, I noticed she was skittish. I reached out to push a strand of hair away from her face and she flinched, as if she thought I was going to strike her. I asked her if there was anyone who hit her, and she said no, I'd just startled her. I could tell she was lying. After that, I tried to make it a point of staying in touch. Over the next four years, between the times I saw her at Grandma's and when Emily ran away, she began to open up to me a bit. She alluded to the fact that her father was very strict and not one to spare the rod. She never used the word *beating* until the last phone call, just before she ran away, although I suspected she'd been disciplined aggressively for most of her life. I should have done more to help her. Now I'm terrified it might be too late."

I wanted to reassure Nicole that it wasn't too late, that we'd find Emily happy and healthy and ready to reunite with her, but I doubted that was true.

"Had Emily ever run away before?" Jack asked.

"Not that I know of. But then, I wasn't close enough to her or our mother to know whether she had."

"Had Emily ever mentioned Slayer to you before the call letting you know she was running away with him?" Jack wondered.

Nicole shook her head. "No. Most of our contact was via text. The messages were short and to the point. I'd ask her how school was, and she'd say fine. I'd ask if she'd had a nice birthday or Christmas and she'd say it was fine. We never discussed anything of substance, though I wanted her to know I was there for her if she needed me."

"And the last time you spoke to her? Before she ran away. Did she call or text?" I asked.

"She called."

"Why do you think she called you?" I asked.

Nicole frowned. "I'm not sure. I guess she knew she was leaving for good and wanted to be sure I understood why. Maybe she was scared about the decision she'd made and I was some sort of lifeline." Nicole shook her head. "I really don't know why she called. She could have texted if she just wanted me to know. Maybe she wanted to hear my voice, or maybe she needed to feel she had a plan B if things didn't work out with Slayer."

Jack sat back in his chair, deep in thought. At last, he said, "Okay, so Emily called and told you she was running away, and you made the arrangements for her to send you a selfie every week. Then what?"

Nicole looked down at her hands. "And then I waited for the photos to arrive. The first one came on March 20. Another came every Monday through May 8. I didn't receive a photo on May 15 or ever again."

"Did you speak to Emily after she called to tell you she was running away? Did you ever text or respond to a photo?"

Nicole looked up. I could see the regret in her eyes. "No. I didn't do anything. I should have. Maybe Emily wouldn't be missing if I had."

"Prior to Emily missing the selfie for Monday, May 15, did you report Emily as a runaway to the police, contact your mother, or try to get in touch with any of her friends?" Jack rattled off.

Nicole shook her head.

He took a moment, then continued. "Emily had been sending photos once a week and then stopped. What did you do at that point?"

"At first nothing," Nicole said. "I wasn't even that worried when she missed the first Monday. Things happen. When you're on the move, sometimes the days of the week become all tangled up." Nicole sounded as if she knew that for a fact. I supposed she did. I wouldn't be a bit surprised to learn she'd spent time on the move when she left her last foster home. "It was when she missed the second Monday that I began to worry. I sent her a text, but it didn't go through. As I said last night, I tried to report her missing, but that got me nowhere. When I hadn't heard from Emily in a month, I went to Bangor and tried to speak to my mother. She told me to mind my own business and closed the door in my face. I went to Emily's high school, trying to find a friend or teacher she might have been in touch with, but I was told she'd stopped going to class months before she ran away, and she didn't appear to have any friends. I knew she'd met this Slayer in a bar, so I went to a few and asked around. I found out Slayer was part of a band that sometimes played in the area, but the word was it had broken up right about the time he and Emily took off."

"And then?" Jack asked in a matter-of-fact tone.

"And then I went home. I worried and stewed for a few weeks, then decided to try to follow the places Emily had been to figure out where she might have been heading. The minute I began, I saw how difficult that task would be. The selfies were all taken in hard-to-identify places. A wall, a door, a forest with no geographic markers to rely on. I looked for two months with no luck, then, eventually, I figured out where this one was taken." Nicole slipped a photo across the table to us. It was of the same girl we'd seen standing in front of the old cabin six, this time standing in front of a brown door with what looked like columns with crosses at the top. To the left of the door, behind where Emily was standing, were bricks.

"You identified the location from this photo?" I asked. It seemed unlikely.

"It took me a while because all I really had was a brown door, but the pattern in it was unique and seemed familiar. I had a feeling I'd seen it before, but I couldn't remember where. Finally, it came to me in the middle of the night. The door I vaguely remembered was to the Salem Witch Museum. I'd visited it a few years earlier, and I went back again with the photo to confirm my suspicion. The pattern on the door matched the pattern in the photo exactly. Once I was sure, I began asking people in Salem if they'd seen her."

"And did you find someone who had?" I asked.

Nicole lifted a shoulder. "I began my search by talking to staff and volunteers at the museum, but that got me nowhere. It had been a while, and a lot of visitors pass through. Not a single person recognized her, and I was about to give up when I decided to stop for lunch. I went into a small café nearby and was looking at the menu when the waitress made a comment about the photo of Emily, which was on the table in front of me. I asked if she'd seen the girl and she said she had. It was July by this time, four months since Emily had taken the photo, but the waitress had spoken to her and said she remembered her. I explained who I was and why I was looking for her, and the waitress gave me some ideas that helped me find the location of the next photo."

I sat forward just a bit. "Did the waitress say whether Emily was alone?"

"She said she seemed to be, but she also said Emily told her that she was traveling with a friend who had some business to take care of, so she was doing some sightseeing while she waited. She never told the waitress her friend's name. What she did say was that she and her friend were heading south. Emily claimed not to know the exact route or timeline involved in their journey, but she said she hoped to be able to visit Atlantic City. I scoured the photos that came later, comparing them to photos of Atlantic City on the internet. It took me several days, but eventually, I realized the April 17 photo looked like it could have been taken on the boardwalk. I traveled to New Jersey and walked up and down the boardwalk with my photo. I finally matched it to a building that houses the Warner Theater, among other things."

I knew the place; I'd visited Atlantic City a time or two myself. "And did you find someone who remembered seeing Emily in New Jersey?"

Nicole shook her head. I couldn't help but notice the fatigue in her eyes. "Not at first. The boardwalk is a busy place, with a lot of visitors every day, and it had been over four months since the photo had been sent to me by then. I spent a week in Atlantic City, walking up and down the boardwalk, showing Emily's photo to anyone who would look at it. I was about to give up when a woman who was working in a trinket shop, telling fortunes, stopped me. She identified herself as Gilda, no last name, and said she'd seen Emily in April. Apparently, it was a slow day in the store, so she chatted with her when she came in to look around. Gilda said she'd picked up on the fact that Emily was in some sort of trouble. She claimed she tried to warn Emily that she needed to watch her back, but Emily shrugged it off."

Jack looked at the photo Emily had sent from the boardwalk and studied it intently. "Did the fortune teller say what sort of trouble she feared Emily was in?"

"No. To be honest, I wasn't interested in some vision she tried to convince me she'd had. I wanted cold hard facts. I wanted to find my sister. Just as the waitress I spoke to in Salem told me, the fortune teller said Emily was alone, and again, Emily claimed she was traveling with a friend who had business to take care of, so she was sightseeing. As before, she didn't mention her friend's name or give any details about their business. The fortune teller said Emily appeared happy and relaxed on the surface, but she could sense a wariness. She hid it well, but Gilda was certain Emily was troubled, even frightened to an extent."

I took a deep breath and let it out slowly. I knew when we began this journey the outcome could very well be tragic, but the more we learned, the more convinced I was we weren't likely to find a happily ever after when this mystery was solved. The fact that Emily said she was traveling with a friend who never seemed to be around was troubling. What sort of business could this guy be conducting that would cause him to leave her alone for so much of the time?

"Did the fortune teller know where Emily was heading?" I asked.

"South. Again, she was vague, but she did say she and her friend were heading south. I still hadn't identified the location of the March 20, April 3, or April 10 photos then, so I had no way of knowing if they were taking a direct route or zigzagging as they went, but south was a good guess of where I'd find the next location. I asked the fortune teller to look at the other photos to see if she recognized any of them. She thought the one sent on April 24 was also taken in a popular tourist spot. She didn't have an exact location, but she said she could sense a lot of people walking, talking, eating, even screaming."

"Screaming?"

"This is the photo." Nicole handed it to me. Emily was standing in front of a white fence with something yellow in the background. It was very nondescript, and I thought it could have been taken anywhere. "At first, I didn't think there was anything in the photo that would tell me where it might have been taken, but the fortune teller's comment about a lot of people and screaming made me think of an amusement park. I decided to go to Virginia Beach. I'm not sure why. I mean, there are any number of amusements parks south of Atlantic City. It was just a guess."

"Had Emily ever mentioned wanting to visit Virginia Beach?" Jack asked.

"Not that I remembered. When I got there, I walked miles and miles again, trying to find the place that matched the background in the photo."

"And did you find it?"

Nicole nodded. "Before I even left home, I scoured photos of Virginia Beach and found there was a white fence separating the beach from the rides. That fence seemed to match the photo, and of course Virginia Beach is south of Atlantic City, but not so far south that it would be unlikely Emily and Slayer had made the trip there in a week. Not long after I got there, I found a temporary exhibit near the Ferris wheel. It was near the white fence and was the exact shade of yellow as the backdrop of the photo. And Virginia Beach was just the kind of place it seemed Emily was attracted to."

I picked up the photo. It was about as nondescript as you could get. "You must have been really determined to identify Virginia Beach from this."

"I *was* determined. By then it was into September and I was getting desperate. It had been so long since I'd heard from Emily. I was beginning to wonder if she was still alive."

I put my hand over Nicole's. "I can't even imagine going through what you have. To have a loved one missing must be the worst sort of hell one can experience."

Nicole looked down at the photo. "I keep thinking, if something happened to Emily, it will have been my fault. I should have done more. I should have been a better sister."

The three of us were quiet. The momentum of our conversation had lulled as an atmosphere of strong emotion seeped into the cabin. I glanced at Jack.

"So, you found the probable location of that photo and then what?" Jack asked.

"And then I walked what must have been a hundred miles up and down the walkway that parallels the beach, asking everyone I came across if they'd seen Emily. No one had. I was certain this was the right place, but it seemed Emily hadn't spoken to anyone who remembered her. I suppose given the late-summer crowds, that shouldn't have surprised me. Eventually, I went home and tried to pick up a trail that seemed to have gone cold from there. I knew she was most likely heading south and her route had been following the coast so far, but beyond that I had nothing. By the time October rolled around, I was getting even more desperate. I got in touch with my mother one more time but that got me nowhere, and because Emily was classified as a runaway who'd turned seventeen while she was away, none of the law enforcement personnel I spoke to were prepared to help me. I really had hit a dead end."

"And then?" I asked, my heart filled with empathy for Nicole.

"And then nothing for what felt like a long time. I'd spent time and money on my search and was getting nowhere. I was beyond discouraged. Then, in early November, I was scanning the internet looking for inspiration when I came across an article that had been published by the South Carolina Department of Tourism two years prior. There were photos of the top-ten off-the-beaten-track places to relax and unwind on vacation. One of the photos was of the main house at the Turtle Cove Resort on Gull Island. The house you currently live in."

The Gull Island Writers' Retreat had been called the Turtle Cove when Garrett ran it as a family resort.

Nicole pulled out the photo she'd printed off. "If you look at this, you'll see one of the cabins is visible in the background. It isn't number six, but all the old cabins looked pretty much the same, with the same green doors. For the first time in months, I felt I'd found a real clue, so I made the trip to Gull Island to check it out. When I arrived, I found out the resort had been turned into a writers' retreat, and the old cabins either had been torn down or remodeled. I also learned the resort had been temporarily shut down because of the illness of the resort owner, so at the time the photo was taken it was closed. I planned to come out here to talk to whoever was in charge, but this was the last place I knew Emily had been, so I was wary of giving away too much. When I learned you had cabins for rent, I decided to rent one. I figured I could continue with my research while looking around the grounds and the island."

"Did you ever find out where the photos from March 20, April 3, April 10, and May 1 were taken?" Jack asked.

"Some of them. But not until after I came to Gull Island. I've never stopped looking for her. You've probably noticed I haven't always been here."

"Have you shown Emily's photo around town?" I asked.

"Selectively. I'm not sure why, but by the time I came here, I had it in my head that someone on Gull Island was responsible for Emily's disappearance. I'm not the sort to trust easily. In fact, my experience has been that most people aren't worthy of trust, and if you let them in, they'll let you down." Nicole looked directly at me. "I'm sorry about the way I treated you. The way I've treated everyone."

I put my hand over hers. "It's okay. Really. What we need to do now is to focus on finding Emily."

Nicole went on to explain that since she'd been living on Gull Island she'd identified the April 10 photo as being taken in New Haven, Connecticut, and the photo from May 1 was taken in Wrightsville Beach, North Carolina. I'd confirmed a clear pattern of a southerly route along the coastline. Now all we needed to do was to figure out where Emily went after leaving here. It had been almost nine months since the May 8 photo was taken. If Emily wasn't dead, she could be anywhere by now.

Chapter 3

"So, what do you think?" I asked Jack as we drove to the newspaper. It had started to drizzle, adding an extra layer of dreariness to the day. Still, Gull Island on a dreary day was a lot cozier than anywhere I'd ever lived before.

"I wish I could say we have some good leads and I feel confident our search for Emily will be successful, but I'm worried we have too little to go on given the amount of time that's passed. Nine months is a long time. Even if Emily lost her phone or became distracted and didn't remember to call her sister on time, in nine months you'd think she could have found a way to contact her. She had to know Nicole would be worried about her."

"Yeah, it doesn't look good. But Nicole wants to know what happened to Emily one way or the other, and I want to help her."

Jack put his hand over mine and gave it a squeeze. "I know. Me too. We have copies of all Nicole's notes, maps, and photos. Let's spread everything out when we get to the newspaper and come up with a strategy."

I glanced out the window as we drove through the little seaside town. The main commercial area was a charming village of mom-and-pop shops that met the needs of both visitors and residents. I'd made quite a few friends since moving to the island and knew the merchants who depended on weekend visitors from the larger cities nearby would be hoping for a return of sunny skies even more than I. I turned back to Jack to share the thought that had been nagging at me. "It seems to me that we need to decide whether to head north to retrace Emily's steps from the time she left home, or start here, at the last place she was seen, and try to figure out where she went next."

Jack pulled into the small parking area behind the newspaper office. "Given the amount of time since Emily's last contact with Nicole, we should probably try to pick up the trail here and try to move forward. It seems unlikely anything we might manage to pick up along her journey from Maine to South Carolina would give us any solid information about what happened to her after she arrived on the island."

I climbed out of Jack's truck and let Kizzy hop down from the backseat. Jack used his key to unlock the door, then stepped back so Kizzy and I could enter first. I clicked on the lights and Jack tossed the stack of folders and files on the table. I began to organize the things Nicole had given us while Jack made a pot of coffee. Kizzy headed to the sofa that was butted up against one wall. She stuck her head under one of the cushions, then pulled out her stuffed moose. I guess she knew exactly where she'd left it.

Once she had it, she trotted over to her bed and curled up with it. Jack tossed her a dog biscuit, which she happily began to nibble on.

Once the coffee was ready, Jack poured us each a cup and sat down across the table from me. Nicole had gone to the police on a couple of occasions with zero luck, but as far as I knew, she hadn't spoken to Deputy Rick Savage here on the island. I'd stop by his office later that afternoon, fill him in, and ask if he had any suggestions on how we should best proceed. "Okay. Where do we start?"

Jack repeatedly tapped his pen against his notepad. "I feel like we should try to identify the man Emily was traveling with. Nicole said he called himself Slayer, but she didn't seem to have any other details about him. Chances are finding out what he was up to could be the key to figuring out what happened to them."

"I've been wondering what sort of business he was conducting as they traveled south. That could be the key. I'd be surprised if it was anything legal."

"Maybe we can track down the bar where Slayer and Emily met. The bartender or one of the regulars might know what they were up to."

Jack looked down at his notes. "I'd like to fill in the holes in Nicole's timeline. There are," Jack paused to count, "two photos with unidentified locations: March 20 and April 3. It may not be important to know the exact route she took, but it couldn't hurt to dig around a bit."

"It occurred to me that we should bring Rick in on this," I said, voicing my earlier thought. "I know you have work to do today, but I could stop by his office, and then maybe head over to Gertie's. She always seems to know what's going on even when no one else does."

Jack stood and began gathering up the photos and notes. "Sounds like a plan. You can use my truck. I should be done here by the time you finish talking to them. We'll grab a bite to eat and firm up our plans this evening."

******

When Rick Savage and I first met, he wasn't a fan of what he referred to as my *bullheaded refusal to stay out of police matters.* Since he began dating Vikki and we've solved several cold cases together, our relationship has evolved. I guess you could say I've started to grow on him. Most of the time, we get on just fine, and more often than not, he's happy to see me when I pop into his office without notice. Today, he was out on a call when I arrived. His receptionist assured me that he would be back in about an hour, so I headed over to Gertie's on the Wharf for some down-home conversation and a snack to tide me over until my dinner with Jack.

Gertie's was located on the long wharf that jutted into the marina where fishing boats loaded and unloaded their catch each day. The wharf wasn't far from the resort, which meant that, coupled with the exceptional company one often found there, I was a frequent customer. The small restaurant was decorated in a nautical motif that was completely appropriate given the wall of windows that ran down one side and along the back looking out over the harbor, dotted with colorful boats. Gertie did a booming summer business, but during the winter, the restaurant, like the island, had a slower pace and a more relaxed atmosphere.

"Morning, Gertie," I said as I entered the warm, sweet-smelling café. The place was deserted because it was late for the breakfast crowd and early for the gang who came in for lunch. That suited me fine; I preferred to speak with her without having an audience to take into consideration.

"Morning, darling. Been hoping you'd stop by. Can't help but wonder how that young'un and those kids she's raising are doing. Heard she spent some time in the hospital."

I sat down at the counter and Gertie slid a cup of coffee in front of me. "Abby is doing all right, considering. Things have been hard on her, but she's a strong young woman, and I think in the long run she'll be just fine. We've asked her to stay with us at the resort until after the baby's born."

Gertie crossed her arms over her ample bosom. "Glad to hear it. There are some folks who seem to attract more than their share of troubles, and it seemed as if Abby is one of 'em. You want something to eat to go with that coffee?"

"Maybe a muffin."

"Banana nut or cranberry? I have cinnamon scones and apple turnovers too."

"A cranberry muffin would be great."

Gertie topped off my coffee, then went into the kitchen for the muffin. When she returned, I launched right in to my reason for being there. I showed Gertie the photo of Emily standing in front of the old cabin six and asked if she'd ever seen her.

"Yeah, I seen her."

I raised a brow. "When?"

Gertie paused, tapping her finger against her chin a few times. "I guess it was in the spring. She came in looking like something the dog done drug in. She was a cute little thing. Had the most sorrowful eyes, but a sweet, sweet smile. She showed up that first time with a handful of coins, mostly nickels and dimes. She asked if it was enough to buy a cup of coffee. It wasn't quite, but I gave her a cup. When I heard her stomach rumble, I gave her breakfast too."

"Did you talk to her?"

"Honey, you know Gertie talks to everyone who comes in here."

I couldn't argue with that. "Do you remember what you talked about?"

Gertie picked up an empty coffee cup that had been left by an earlier customer and put it in the bin of dishes to be washed, then began to wipe the counter. "She said her name was Emily, told me that she'd come south with a friend. Seems the friend had dropped her off at some cabin they were staying in but hadn't come back. She said there was no food in the kitchen, and she'd just spent the last of her money on the coffee. She wondered if I knew of anyone who might have a temporary job."

I rested my forearms on the counter and leaned slightly forward. "And did you?"

"Of course. You know Gertie isn't the sort to turn her back on an injured fawn like that little girl appeared to be. It looked like the child had attempted to wash up, but she was wearing dirty clothes, and for some God Almighty reason she'd added thick blue streaks to her lovely hair. I told her I could use some help and wouldn't mind paying for it, but she'd need to lose the streaks and find some clean clothes. She said she didn't have any, or a way to wash the clothes she had, and the streaks were from a permanent dye. The poor little thing looked like a scared rabbit, so I took her over to Betty Sue, who agreed to work on the blue hair. I stopped off at the secondhand store and left some money so Emily could pick out some new duds when she was finished at the beauty salon and told her to come back here after she got herself cleaned up and I'd find some work for her to do."

Emily didn't have blue streaks in her hair in the May 8 selfie, so I surmised she'd visited the salon before she took the photo. "And did you find work for her to do?"

Gertie nodded. "She came back that same day. She worked real hard and I paid her what I could. I was fine with her sticking around, but a few days after she first wandered in, she was gone."

"Do you know where she went?"

Gertie leaned back against the counter behind her. "Why exactly are you asking all these questions?"

"She's Nicole Carrington's sister." I took a few minutes to bring Gertie up to speed.

Gertie made a clicking sound with her tongue and shook her head. "I knew that little girl was in trouble. Talked to Rick about her after she disappeared. He said I shouldn't worry, that it sounded like she was a drifter who'd gone on her way. I thought different, though. That little girl was in trouble. I could see it in her eyes."

"Did she ever tell you specifically where she was staying, who she was with, where she was heading?"

Gertie slowly shook her head. "She just said her friend had gotten them a cabin. Lots of cabins in this area, and I didn't think to ask exactly where this cabin was located. Based on the photo you done brought with you, though, I'm guessing they were squatting out at the resort while Garrett was in the hospital."

"It seems that might have been the case. Unfortunately, cabin six, the cabin in the photo, is one of the ones I had torn down during the remodel. Any clues or evidence that might have been there is long gone."

"Shame, that's what that is."

I had to agree. "Do you know if the friend Emily mentioned ever came back? You said he'd dropped her off a couple of days before she first came in here but hadn't come back yet."

"Not as far as I know. She did say she and her friend had been traveling together for a while, and I do remember her mentioning him having some business to take care of that caused him to take off for days at a time. But on the last day she worked here, she seemed really upset about something. She wouldn't say what, but I suspected it had something to do with that friend. I could see she was in a bad way, so I told her that she was welcome to work for me for as long as she needed, and if she needed a place to stay, I could arrange for that as well. She seemed genuinely grateful and even enthusiastic about my offers, but I never saw her again."

"And you have no idea where she might have been going after she left Gull Island?"

Gertie shook her head. "Never said where she was heading. I did get the feeling she started out somewhere up north. She talked about there being snow at home. A lot of it."

If Gertie spoke to Rick after Emily disappeared, and he had done some poking around, it was likely he might have more to tell me. It had been an hour since I'd been by his office, so I hoped he'd be back now. I paid Gertie for the coffee and muffin, thanked her for the information, and headed back to the Gull Island branch of the sheriff's department. Before I was even halfway there, I received a call from Garrett, letting me know he and Clara were at the museum visiting with Meg, and they'd uncovered some information I might be interested in. I made a sharp left and headed to the museum.

Meg Collins had lived on the island most of her life. A sweet older woman who knew a lot about the island and its history, she was also the head of the local turtle rescue squad. She might very well have run in to Emily in May.

The museum had been built on a hill, which provided an unobstructed view of the ocean in the distance. During the spring and summer, the colorful flower gardens and well-maintained walkways provided a pleasant place to gaze out at the sea or share a snack at one of the many picnic tables. When I arrived, I found Garrett and Clara sitting at one of the long tables with George and Meg.

"You said you had news?" I asked as I sat down.

"Garrett showed me the photo of Emily," Meg began as she moved it to the center of the table. "He wanted to know if I'd seen her, and I had. It was a while ago, early last spring, but I'm sure she was the young girl I spoke to while checking the nests on the south side of the resort."

"Was she alone?" I asked.

"Yes. When I happened upon her she was sitting on a rock looking out to sea. I said hi, she asked what I was doing, and I told her a bit about the efforts of our little group to ensure that as many baby turtles as possible make it to maturity. She seemed really interested, so I let her tag along while I checked the nests."

"Did she say anything that might help us find her?" I asked. "Who she was with or where they planned to go next?"

"She told me that she'd been traveling with a friend for a while but had grown tired of the constant movement. She was ready to settle somewhere and was considering staying right here on the island. I asked her if she had a place to stay, and she said she'd been staying in a cabin her friend had found, but she knew he'd be ready to move on before too long."

"Did she say anything else?"

"Not really. At least not anything important enough to remember."

"I wonder if Emily told her friend that she'd decided to stay here and he was less than happy about the idea," George said.

"You think he might have hurt her?" I responded.

George tilted his head to the side. "Perhaps. Or he forced her to leave. Maybe he didn't want her running away, so he took her phone."

We were quiet for a moment, and then I looked at Clara, who was staring intently at the photo of Emily. "Are you picking up something?"

Clara's brows furrowed to reveal a deep line of concern.

"What is it?" I asked.

"I do sense something." Clara took my hand in hers. She turned it over so it was palm up and studied it. Her frown grew even deeper.

"What is it?" I asked again. "Do you know what happened to her? Is she in danger?"

Clara shook her head. "No. Not Emily. I do sense danger, however." Clara looked me in the eye. Her gaze was so strong, it sent shivers down my spine. "The danger I'm sensing isn't connected to Emily but to you."

"Me?" I asked in a high, squeaky voice. "Why would I be in danger?"

Clara's eyes grew dark. She took on a far-off stare. While she seemed to be looking into the distance, it occurred to me that she was looking at something only she could see. "Something happened before Emily arrived on Gull Island. Something that altered the course of events. Things aren't as they should have been. If you want to find out what happened to Emily, you'll need to go back to the beginning." Clara focused directly at me again. "The problem is, it's at the beginning that's where the danger you'll encounter resides."

Chapter 4

When I finally got to Rick's office, he was working on an incident report. He motioned for me to take one of the chairs across his desk while he finished up. At last he stopped typing, turned away from his computer, and glanced in my direction. "I could ask why you've stopped by for a visit on this rainy morning, but I think I can guess. It's Tuesday. The group at the retreat meets on Mondays. I'd say you have a new case and you need my help to solve it."

I grinned. "And the deputy wins a kewpie doll."

"So, what long-forgotten mystery has captured the attention of the Mystery Mastermind Group this week?"

"The disappearance of Emily Halliwell."

Rick frowned. "Why does that name sound familiar?"

"Because she was on the island and worked for Gertie for a few days this past May. When Emily disappeared without even bothering to let Gertie know she was leaving, she grew concerned and brought the matter to your attention."

I watched the light go on in Rick's eyes. "Ah, I do remember. A drifter hard on her luck. Seems she was in town with a friend who'd made himself scarce. Gertie, being Gertie, took pity on her and gave her a job."

"That's right."

Rick frowned. "So why are the writers interested in her? I did a database search when Gertie spoke to me. The girl didn't have a record and there was no missing persons report matching her name or description. Seemed she simply moved on."

I settled back and filled Rick in on the whole story, starting with the fact that the missing girl was Nicole's half sister. When I finished my tale, Rick leaned back in his chair, steepling his fingers across his chest.

"I understand why the group might be interested in this case, but after hearing the entire story, I'm still of a mind that the girl just continued on her way. Maybe the boyfriend came back, or maybe she got tired of waiting and left without him."

"Maybe that's what happened, but from what I've learned, Emily had pretty much decided to stay on the island and work for Gertie. She was tired of traveling. She wanted to put down some roots."

"Maybe she changed her mind. Or maybe the boyfriend showed up and sweet-talked her into leaving with him."

"If that was all there was to it, why would she suddenly stop sending the selfies to Nicole?"

"Maybe she lost her phone. Maybe her parents, who were probably paying for it, turned it off. You just finished telling me the girl didn't have two nickels to rub together. If she lost her phone, I doubt she had the cash to replace it."

"If she'd been missing for a week, I might agree with that, but it's been almost nine months. It would seem that in nine months she could have found a way to get hold of her sister."

Rick let out a breath. "You're right. In nine months she could have found a way to contact her sister if she wanted to." He sat forward. "From what you've told me, the sisters weren't close, and I've met this Nicole a time or two. She strikes me as being both pushy and moody. Maybe Emily only agreed to send the selfies to get the girl off her back, or maybe Nicole threatened to report her to the police as a runaway if she didn't. Maybe Emily had finally come to the decision that it wasn't worth the hassle."

I took a moment to consider that. "Maybe that's what happened and maybe it isn't." I looked Rick in the eye. "If you had a sister, wouldn't you want to know for sure?"

Rick nodded. "I would."

"So you'll help me?"

Rick lifted a shoulder. "I'll do what I can. I can run a new search, and the photo you have will come in handy. I didn't have that the first time around. What do we know about the boyfriend?"

"Not a lot, except that Emily met him in a bar. Emily's from Bangor, Maine, so we're assuming that's where she met Slayer. That's all I really know about him."

Rick flattened his forearms on the desk. "Okay. Let me see what I can do. Will you be home this evening?"

"At some point. Jack and I are planning to grab a bite when he finishes work."

"I'm coming by this evening to hang out with Vikki and the kids. If I have any news, I'll let you know then."

I left Rick's office and headed to Betty Boop's Hair Salon. Mayor Betty Sue Bell was the sort who could talk your ear off if you let her. She also had a way of getting the folks in her chair to talk about themselves. Maybe she'd gotten Emily to do that while she was taking care of the blue-streak situation. It couldn't hurt to ask.

"Looks like someone's come in for an emergency wash and trim," Betty, dressed in the loud colors she wore while acting the role of hairdresser, greeted me.

I put my hand to my hair. Sure, it was damp from the rain, but it wasn't that bad. "No, I can't stay. I just had a few questions for you about a case the mastermind group is working on, if you have a couple of minutes."

Betty raised one perfectly shaped brow. "Are you sure you don't want me to give you a quick trim while we chat?"

"I'm sure." I glanced at the other three hairdressers, each with her own client. "Can we speak in the back?"

Betty shrugged. "If you'd like."

I followed her down the hall to the small room in the back that the ladies who worked there used for breaks. Betty sat down at the table and indicated that I should too. I settled myself, then took a moment to decide where to begin the conversation I wanted to have. "I spoke to Gertie this morning," I began. "She told me that she had a temporary employee last spring named Emily. She brought her into the salon so you could remove blue dye from her hair."

"Sure, I remember her. Sweet little thing. I felt real bad for her. Seemed like she might be alone in the world. You said you wanted to speak to me regarding something pertaining to the mastermind group. Is she in some sort of trouble?"

"Maybe." I explained what I knew about Emily's situation, including that she was Nicole's half sister. Betty Sue's smile faded as I detailed the reason for our investigation.

"You know, I suspected something wasn't right about that girl. She tried to make it sound like everything was fine, that her friend had simply been detained, but I could sense there was more to it than she wanted to say."

"Did she tell you anything that might help explain where she went after she left the island? Anything at all about the trip, the man she was with, or the business she said he was doing as they made their way south?"

Betty patted her big hair into place before answering. I swear, it wouldn't surprise me to learn that all the women who worked here went through an entire can of hairspray every single day. No one could keep all that hair piled up on their heads without excessive use of the heavy-duty variety.

"When she first got here with Gertie, I couldn't get her to say more than two words," Betty Sue began. "She was as skittish as a kitten in a house full of dogs. I could see she was terrified."

"Did she give you a hint of what she was worried about?"

Betty Sue shook her head. "She wasn't one to overshare, but it seemed she was worried about the friend she came to the island with. At first, I thought she was worried because he hadn't come back when he was supposed to, but as time went on and we got to chatting, I got the impression she was really scared about something else."

"Something else?"

"She was very careful not to say exactly what was going on. It was more that I picked up on a certain level of fear in her eyes."

"Did she ever mention the name of the person she was with?"

Betty Sue tilted her head. The hair layered on top should have toppled over, but it didn't. "No, not that I recall."

"From what's been said to this point, I'm willing to bet the business Emily's friend was in to was illegal. Maybe drugs, maybe something else. It doesn't seem as if she was involved in it."

"That fits my impression of the situation. She looked to be not only stressed but exhausted. I think the trip that may have started off as an adventure had begun to wear on her. She was as skinny as a pole, so I'm assuming a regular source of nutrition was an issue. She was a very pretty girl, but her fatigue showed in her eyes."

"Do you think she was doing drugs?"

Betty Sue shook her head. "I didn't pick up a drug vibe. It was more of a beaten-down-by-life vibe. I've known others with the same look."

"Do you think she was suicidal?"

"No. Not exactly. I don't think she had plans to hurt herself, but if the opportunity came along for her to just lay down and fade peacefully away, I'm not sure she would have fought it. Of course, I saw her on day one of her employment with Gertie. I've talked to her about it, and she was confident the girl found her will to fight for a better life during the few short days she worked at the restaurant. I think Gertie not only showed her kindness but gave her hope that the world could be a welcoming place." Betty looked toward the front of the salon. "Sounds like my next client is here."

"I won't keep you, but if you think of anything at all that might help us find her, will you call me?"

Betty Sue wrapped me in a hug. "I'll do that. I sure hope you find that little girl. I hate to think of her out there on her own."

"Yeah." I hugged Betty Sue back. "Me too."

******

When Jack and I returned to the resort after dinner, Rick was already there. The entire living room was full as he, Vikki, Garrett, Clara, George, Abby, and all four kids watched a Disney movie that someone must have rented. I waved to them as I walked through the front door. Kizzy trotted over to say hi to the kids, giving me a chance to motion to Rick that he should meet me in the kitchen when he had a chance.

The house was full a lot of the time, even though most of the writers had their own cabins; with four kids added to the pack, it felt more like a home than it ever had. I made a pot of coffee while Jack took

Kizzy out for a quick bathroom break. By the time they returned, Rick had made his way into the kitchen, where he took a seat at the dining table.

"Did you find anything?" I asked, sitting down across from him.

"Yes, I think I did." He reached down to the satchel he'd brought in with him and pulled out a folder. "I started by calling the Bangor PD and speaking to the officer who took Nicole's call when she initially tried to file the missing persons report. He went to speak to Emily's parents, and they assured him Emily wasn't missing but had run away. The parents painted a picture of a teen who was in and out of trouble on a regular basis. The mother even went so far as to say that, before she left, Emily had stolen a hundred dollars that was hidden away for emergencies, and she wanted to press charges if he manage to track her down. The mother indicated Emily was no longer welcome in her home and should be sent to foster care in the event she turned up."

"Can she do that? Can a mother simply say she no longer wants a child and ask that she be turned over to foster care?"

"I'm sure it's more complicated than that; the point is, the officer who looked in to Nicole's call came away with the impression that Emily had run away and was most likely better off for having done so. He never filed an official report of any kind. Emily was almost seventeen and the family situation she ran from was less than ideal."

Poor Emily. My mom drove me crazy, but at least I never got the impression she didn't care about me and didn't want me in her life. "Did you find out anything about Slayer?" I asked.

Rick nodded. He showed me a photo of a thin man with long dark hair and multiple tattoos. "Meet Myron Black, aka Slayer. He's twenty-two years old and had lived in Bangor for just four months prior to leaving, we assume, with Emily. Myron was part of a band called the Swamp Demons. I spoke to the lead guitar, Bryce Payton, whose stage name is Grunge. Payton told me the band broke up shortly before Black left town and he hadn't seen him since. He did say it was his belief Black was heading north, not south."

"Did he know for certain whether Emily was with him?"

"No. He said he'd seen Emily hanging around at gigs, but Black hadn't said anything about heading out with anyone. I asked if he knew why he left town and although he said he wasn't a hundred percent certain, he thought he was meeting a man in Fort Collins, a small town on the Canadian border, about a business opportunity."

"I wonder what sort of business Slayer could have all the way up there," I murmured.

"Payton didn't know, but he suggested it was most likely something illegal."

I sat back in my chair, considering everything Rick had said. The more I learned about this mess, the more certain I was that we weren't likely to find a happily ever after at the end of the road.

"We don't know where the selfie sent to Nicole on March 20 was taken. That was the first Monday Emily was on the road," Jack pointed out. "I suppose they may have headed north initially, met with whoever Slayer planned to see, and then started south."

Rick and I agreed that may very well have been the case.

"Okay, so how does this help us find Emily?" I asked.

"I'm not sure it does," Rick said. "I ran Myron Black through the database and he doesn't have a police record. In fact, I didn't find anything about him. It appears he's been skating by under the radar."

"So we still have nothing." I groaned.

"We don't have a lot," Rick agreed, "but now that we have photos of both Emily and the man we believe to have been her traveling companion, we can circulate them together, and maybe something will pop."

I hoped Rick was right. I wanted to be able to give Nicole her answers, but I hated to be the bearer of bad news.

Rick went back to the movie and I looked at Jack. "I could be off-base, but it feels important to know whether Slayer and Emily actually did go to Fort Collins, and if they did, who they met and why. I have a sense that if we can figure out what it was Slayer was doing as they worked their way south, it might tell us what happened on Gull Island. It sounds like the journey really began in that small border town."

Even as I said that, I remembered Clara's words: *If you want to find out what happened to Emily, you'll need to go back to the beginning. The problem is, it's at the beginning that the danger you'll encounter resides.* I'd decided not to mention my conversation with Clara to Jack. He might hesitate to do what was necessary if he suspected I was in any sort of danger. Clara was occasionally dead-on with her predictions, but just as often, she was wrong.

"So what do you think?" I said. "Should we go to Maine and start looking under rocks?"

"I don't think Emily is hiding under a rock, but a quick trip up there might not be a bad idea." Jack took out his phone and pulled up a map of Maine. "We'd have to fly into LaGuardia and then catch a commuter flight to Bangor. We can rent a car there and drive the rest of the way. I can get away on Thursday. We can plan to spend a couple of nights, which should give us time to look around."

"I can be away Thursday and Friday nights." I looked at Kizzy. "I'll ask Vikki and the other writers if they'd be willing to keep an eye on you because we're flying instead of driving. I know Vikki plans to stay close to home as long as she has Abby and the kids to look out for, so it shouldn't be a problem for two days."

"Okay. You arrange doggy care and I'll book the flight and arrange for a room and a rental car. I've never been that far north in Maine. I'm actually looking forward to getting a look at the place."

"I'm sure there'll be snow. A lot of it. I'll need to dig out my heavy boots. Hopefully, they're in the back of my closet somewhere and didn't end up in the Goodwill bag I dropped off shortly after I arrived on the island."

Chapter 5

Thursday, February 1

Jack booked us an early flight out of Charleston, so I decided to spend the night at his place on Wednesday night, eliminating the need for him to pick me up before anyone else at the resort would be awake the next morning. Nicole had gone chasing after a potential sighting in Florida, so George and I had teamed up the previous day while Jack was working to take Emily and Slayer's photos around town, hoping someone had seen one or both of them. Several Gull Island residents reported having seen Emily the previous spring. Some remembered seeing her around town, while others saw her at Gertie's. Not a single person, though, remembered seeing Slayer, and with all his tats and piercings, he was the sort of person who tended to be noticed. I wondered if

Slayer had stayed on the island at all after he'd dropped Emily at the cabin.

I'd hoped our canvassing would get us at least some of the answers we needed. I still hadn't told Jack what Clara had said about the supposed danger I could be putting myself in by making the trip, but George had heard every word, and throughout the day he'd tried to talk me out of going. I'll admit there was a small voice in the back of my mind nagging at me to be careful, not to take Clara's warning lightly. It wasn't that I was some sort of thrill seeker who snubbed her nose at the very idea of danger; it was more that there was a second voice reminding me the answer to the question of what had happened to Emily Halliwell would most likely be found by going back to where her journey had started. And that was in Bangor.

We'd left Kizzy with Vikki on Wednesday night. I hoped taking care of a pregnant woman, four kids, and a puppy wouldn't be too much for my previously commitment-free friend, but she seemed happy to add the puppy to the mix, and the kids adored Kizzy. When I was ready to leave, Abby's girls had been arguing about whose bed the pup was going to sleep on and who got to take her out for her walk when the time came.

Somehow, despite the short lead time, Jack managed to get us first-class seats, and the trip from Charleston to LaGuardia was fairly pleasant.

"Mimosa?" the flight attendant offered shortly after we boarded.

"Absolutely." Jack accepted two glasses from the tray before I could answer.

"Champagne at six o'clock in the morning?" I raised a brow.

Jack shrugged as he handed me one of the flutes. "I know this is a working trip, but it's still a vacation from our normal lives, so we may as well enjoy the perks that come with these first-class seats."

I took a sip of the bubbly beverage. It did taste wonderful, and Jack was right, this trip was a departure from the everyday. Working trip or not, we might as well enjoy it. "I'm looking forward to our visit to Maine despite the less-than-pleasant reason for it," I said. "I've been to coastal Maine, but I've never visited the interior, and I've certainly never traveled as far north as Fort Collins."

"I made the drive to Montreal once and took the meandering route through Maine, but it was during the summer, and I turned west before I got to the northern border. I'm sure the scenery is going to be vastly different in the winter than it was that summer, but I do remember it being quite breathtaking."

"I'd love to go on a long road trip sometime. I've been a lot of places, but I've always flown, so I haven't had the opportunity to experience the backroads of America. I hear there are some absolutely beautiful places that can only be experienced from a car or on foot."

Jack tipped his glass toward me. "Anytime you want to go on a road trip, I'd be pleased to take you."

"Have you done a lot of road traveling?" I asked as the kid sitting behind me began kicking the back of my seat. I turned to give him the evil eye, but he grinned mischievously and kicked even harder. I decided to ignore him and returned my attention to Jack. Hopefully, the boy would grow tired of the game because his mother, who hadn't looked up once from the magazine she was thumbing through, didn't seem to have a clue what was going on.

Jack shook his head. "Not really. Like you, I usually fly to my destinations. I took a road trip through the south with a friend when I was in college. Talk about an amazing place to visit. The bayous look exactly the way you think they should, with murky water teeming with life just beneath the surface. We were able to see alligators, snakes, turtles, fish, and a variety of insects in and around the water. And the dense trees are amazing. It's sort of frightening but also enchanting."

"Enchanting?"

"It's dark, and the moss hanging down from the trees creates a veil that some say shields the magic that resides in the shadows."

"That's very poetic."

"The bayou is a poetic place. It's teeming with life and mystery. It's a definite must-do at some point in your life."

"It sounds like you and your friend had an awesome trip."

"We did. Louisiana is a beautiful state, and the desert states along the Mexican border are not only very beautiful but also rich with history and culture."

The flight attendant stopped to offer us coffee. I accepted, but Jack declined. The flight offered breakfast, but we'd decided to skip the less-than-appealing eggs and eat a real meal once we landed.

"So, what was your favorite experience on your trip?" I asked as I handed my empty flute to the flight attendant after she brought my coffee.

"There were a lot of really spectacular sights, but I guess my overall favorite was hiking in Carlsbad Caverns."

My eyes grew wide. "That sounds amazing."

Jack wound his fingers through mine. "It was. I can't even describe it."

"I'd love to go sometime."

Jack grinned. "Suddenly, I'm overcome with a desire to experience all that our country has to offer with you by my side. We should definitely plan a trip. I'll buy a motor home so we can bring Kizzy."

"I can probably get away, but what about the newspaper?"

Jack tilted his head, considering. "I've been thinking about hiring some full-time staff. I love my little paper, but I'm not sure I want to be so tied down to it that I can't travel or enjoy other experiences. I can do a lot from the road, and what I can't do via the internet can be done by anyone with a level of specialized training."

"It would be fun to drive from coast to coast. And I'd love to experience the national parks scattered across the country."

"It's settled, then. We'll plan a trip. Maybe even this summer."

"Fall," I countered. "I'd like to go in the fall."

We changed the subject to the present adventure as we flew north. We arrived at LaGuardia in time to grab some breakfast before we had to catch our flight for the second leg of our journey. In the spirit of combining relaxation with our mission, I threw calorie counting to the winds and ordered the eggs Benedict.

"This is fabulous." I groaned with delight as I slowly used my knife and fork to cut the egg-and-sauce-laden biscuit on my plate.

"It's surprising how good the food is at a lot of the airports I've visited. I remember being snowed in at O'Hare for two days during a major blizzard. I was on standby for any available flight once the snow stopped, so I hated to leave, but the VIP lounge was very comfortable, and the food was quite good. In fact, I made a game of it and ate my way from one end of the airport to the other."

"Sounds awful to be stuck for so long."

Jack shrugged. "It wasn't that bad. I had my laptop and managed to get a lot of writing done when I wasn't feeding my face."

"I wonder if it will be snowing on the drive from Bangor to Fort Collins."

"I'm afraid it's likely," Jack answered. "I overheard the flight attendants talking on the trip here, and it sounded like we're in for some weather before we even reach Bangor."

I took a sip of my coffee. "Well, snow is to be expected this time of year. I hope our flight isn't delayed. I've never spent two whole days in an airport, but I've spent more than my share of time in airports waiting to be rebooked after canceled flights, chasing my mother around the country when I was younger. It isn't something I'd care to repeat."

"You visited your mother when she was filming movies?"

"When I was in my teens and early twenties. I don't know why I bothered. She never made all that much of an effort to spend time with me once I got there, but I guess I was idealistic enough in those days to believe it was important to spend holidays and special times with family."

Jack put his hand over mine. "I'm sorry. That sounds rough."

I shrugged. "I had a few bad moments and threw myself more than a couple of pity parties, but I'm over it now. It's been a very long time since I rearranged my life to accommodate my mother." I glanced at my watch. "If the weather is bad up north, we might want to get to the gate early. If we're going to be delayed, it would be best to figure out how that's going to affect our drive from Bangor to Fort Collins. How long is it under ideal weather conditions?"

"I checked, and the drive is more than four hours even without snow. I guess we'll have to play it by ear when we land in Maine. Would you like another cup of coffee?"

"No, I'm finished. Let's head over to the gate and try to find out what we can expect."

As it turned out, the flight to Bangor hit major turbulence at about the halfway point. I consider myself a veteran flyer, but I still tense up when the ride gets bumpy.

"Are you okay?" Jack asked when the plane dipped sharply.

"Not really. I'm definitely not a fan of the bumpy stuff."

Jack reached over and placed a hand on my thigh. "I'm sure the pilot will get us out of this as soon as possible."

I grabbed his arm. "I hope so." I looked out the window, but we were flying through a thick cloud bank that seemed to completely engulf us. "I've flown through a storm a time or two, but it isn't something I enjoy."

Jack had just started to tell me about a book he'd been reading, I think to distract me, when the plane rose sharply, then sank as quickly as it had risen. I stifled a scream, then closed my eyes. By the time we landed I was a bundle of nerves. Jack seemed to have taken the turbulence in stride, but I was pretty sure his arm would never be the same after thirty minutes of my nails digging into his skin as I clung to him for comfort.

"That isn't an experience I want to repeat any time soon," I said once we were safely on the ground.

Jack handed me my overnight bag from the overhead bin. "It was a bit bumpy. I have a feeling the storm is going to be even more intense than we anticipated. I hope the rental agency has the heavy-duty, four-wheel-drive I requested."

I slung my bag over my shoulder and headed to the front of the plane. "I suppose if the storm is really bad we can stop along the way and wait it out."

"I don't think there are a lot of places to stop between Bangor and Fort Collins. Let's grab our rental and then assess the situation. We could always stay in Bangor tonight and get an early start north tomorrow. I don't think it would be a good idea to still be on the road once the sun sets."

As predicted, once we left the terminal we could confirm that the snow was coming down hard, the wind creating whiteout conditions. The car rental agency had a full-size Ford Expedition with four-wheel-drive and a decent ground clearance, but we decided to err on the side of caution and stay in Bangor overnight. Jack managed to find us a lodge-style property at the edge of town that I fell in love with at first sight. Not only was there a two-story fireplace in the lobby, but our room had its own fireplace as well.

"Wow, this is so quaint and cozy," I said as I set my bag on a chair. The king-size bed was piled high with down pillows and fluffy comforters, and the view out a nearby window was of a frozen lake surrounded by dense forest. "If we weren't on such a tight schedule, I could definitely stay here a few days."

Jack lit a match and tossed it onto the fire, which had already been built, while I wandered into the bathroom, which had a shower large enough for two, as well as a Jacuzzi tub with a window looking out onto a private deck. Of course, the deck was buried in snow, so we wouldn't be making use of it, but I imagined in the spring and fall the deck, which overlooked the lake, must be one of the main features of this room.

"The desk clerk told me that they serve wine and light appetizers in the lobby near the fireplace from four to five-thirty, and dinner is served in the dining room from six to eight," Jack informed me. "Or, if you prefer, we can go into town and look for somewhere to eat."

I sat down on the side of the bed and bounced up and down a few times. "It's only two o'clock. Do you think that as long as the storm is forcing us to spend the night here, we should use the time," I looked around the romantic setting of the room, "or at least part of the time, to try to find additional information about Emily and Slayer?"

Jack walked over to the window and looked out. "I doubt it will do us much good to speak to Emily's parents, and I seem to remember Rick saying Slayer's friend Grunge didn't actually live in Bangor, but I suppose it wouldn't hurt to check out the bar where the couple met. We can have a drink, talk to anyone who's around, and still be back in time for dinner here."

"Sounds good. Just give me a few minutes to freshen up."

Jack called down to the desk and got directions to the bar Rick had told us about on Tuesday. The trip, while less than ten miles, took almost thirty minutes due to the heavy snow and the need to drive with caution. Jack parked near the door and we hurried inside, out of the frigid air.

"Can I help you?" the tired-looking man working the bar asked.

"A couple of beers on draft," Jack answered.

I looked around the dark, windowless room while we waited for our drinks. I was sure the place must be hopping in the evenings, when a band played from the raised platform in the corner, but now, in the middle of the afternoon, it was downright depressing.

Jack paid for the drinks, tipping the man generously. He then slipped the photos of Slayer and Emily onto the bar. "My friend and I are in town looking for information on these two. I understand they both frequented this place in the past."

He looked at the photos. "Yeah, I recognize them. The guy goes by the name of Slayer and the girl hung around when he had a gig. Are you working with the cop who called a couple of days ago?"

"We are," Jack verified. "The girl hasn't been seen or heard from since last spring and her sister is worried about her. Can you tell me anything about either of them?"

The bartender set a shot glass on the bar, poured a shot of something dark, and took a drink before he answered. If he drank that way all through his shift, he was going to be hammered by the end of the evening, but that wasn't my problem.

"The guy used to be in a band. He and his buddy Grunge and a couple of backup players did gigs for a while. Then I heard they broke up last winter. I haven't seen Slayer or the girl since. I gave the cop I spoke to contact information for Grunge. I don't know if he followed up."

"Grunge told Deputy Savage that Slayer planned to head north to Fort Collins."

He picked up a toothpick and popped it into his mouth. "Sounds about right. I know Slayer used to have a source for prescription meds from Canada. He'd head north a couple of times a year. I wouldn't be surprised if the girl tagged along. She looked like a lost soul who met Slayer and clamped on for the long haul."

"Do you happen to know the name of Slayer's source?" Jack asked.

He shook his head. "Never said." He took down the same bottle he had drunk from before and poured himself another shot. He tipped it back, then set the empty glass down on the counter.

"I know this is none of my business," I found myself saying, "but if you keep drinking like that, won't you be drunk before your shift is over?"

The man laughed. "Nah. I just need a few to chase away yesterday's hangover. Nothing better for a hangover than a couple of shots of the good stuff."

"Good to know," I mumbled, wondering why someone would want to live their life in a constant state of inebriation.

"You know," the bartender said, "there is someone you might want to speak to. His name is Wader and he lives just outside of Fort Collins. I don't have a phone number or address for him, but Slayer mentioned him a time or two. I think they were friends."

"His last name is Wader?" Jack asked.

"Nickname, on account of him always wading into one sort of trouble or another. If you're inclined to make the trip north, someone can probably point you in his direction."

"Thank you." Jack handed him a fistful of bills. "You've been very helpful." Jack pulled out a business card and gave him that too. "If you think of anything else or run into anyone who might be willing to provide information that will help us track them down, call me."

The bartender grinned as he counted the bills. "Sure thing. Good luck."

"Does everyone in Maine have a weird nickname?" I asked as we headed back through the snow to the SUV.

Jack laughed. "It would seem. Slayer, Grunge, Wader. Although I think it's the sort of person we're dealing with rather than the state where they happen to live." Jack opened the door for me and I slid inside. After he got behind the wheel, he turned and looked at me. "Is there anywhere else you'd like to go before we head back to the lodge?"

"No. I've been thinking about that cozy room with the spectacular view and wonderful fireplace ever since we left it." I yawned, reaching my hands over my head. "I'm pretty tired. I might take a nap before we go down to dinner."

Jack smiled. "I just might join you."

Chapter 6

Friday, February 2

The morning dawned cloudy but free of snow, at least for the time being. The forecast was for additional snow that day, but only flurries rather than the frozen precipitation that had fallen the day before. We got up at the crack of dawn after Jack suggested we get an early start, but I felt relaxed and well rested. The lodge had been lovely. I hoped to return in the future, when long, lazy days and passionate nights would be the only things on the agenda.

"As long as the weather holds, we should be in Fort Collins in time for lunch," Jack commented. "We'll check into the motel, then look around town. Hopefully, someone will recognize Emily, or at least Slayer. Based on what the bartender said, it sounded like Slayer was a regular visitor."

"I wonder if we should stop to speak to local law enforcement as well. It seems a guy like Slayer might have come to their attention at some point."

The car slowed as we approached a plow plodding along at five miles an hour in front of us. I hoped there'd be a place to pass before long or we were in for a slow trip. Despite the lovely scenery, I was anxious to get to Fort Collins. I was about to say something about frustrating delays when I glanced at Jack. He was smiling, his face free of tension, unconcerned by the agonizingly slow progress. I'd noticed in the months we'd known each other that Jack seemed to have the ability to accept the inevitable frustrations he dealt with in his life. I supposed the ability to live in and enjoy the moment was to be envied.

******

Fort Collins was a cute little town I was sure was charming during the summer months, when visitors most likely wandered along the main thoroughfare poking through the shops that were arranged to pull the visitor in. Jack drove straight to the motel he had booked, which, while not as lovely as the lodge, was clean and well maintained and provided its own rustic charm.

We dropped off our belongings in our room and freshened up a bit, then headed out to find a place for lunch. The small café we chose was decorated like a mountain retreat, and while the tables were worn and the booth seats taped in places, it had a certain charm I found welcoming.

"I'm starving," I said as the waitress handed us menus that looked as if they'd been printed a decade before. "What's good here?"

"Everything. If you like soup, we have broccoli cheese today. We have a lunch special that includes a bowl of the soup with your choice of sandwich. We also have a selection of burgers, and salads if you're looking for something lighter."

"A bowl of the soup with a turkey sandwich sounds great," I said.

"I'll have the same, only make my sandwich roast beef," Jack said.

After the waitress left, Jack got up, pulled some change from his pocket, and slipped it into the old-fashioned jukebox tucked away in a corner. The selection of songs was limited to hits from the seventies, but combined with the homey feel of the café, the music seemed perfect. I glanced out the window, which looked out on to the street. It was snowing, but so far, it was gently drifting to the ground at a pace that wouldn't result in much additional accumulation.

"I noticed we passed the police station on our way to the motel," Jack said when he returned to the table. "I think we should stop by after we eat. We can ask our questions, see if they have information that might help us, and formulate a plan from there. Unfortunately, we lost our poking-around time by not making it into town yesterday."

I took a sip of my water. "I agree it will be best to speak to the police first. They might have had run-ins with Slayer, and they might be able to tell us where to find Wader." I glanced to the counter, where the waitress was taking a to-go order. "I wonder if it would be worth our while to show Emily's photo around a bit."

"Maybe, but if there was something illegal going on, perhaps it's best to speak to the police first. Find out who they think Slayer's contact might have been. If there's someone who knows what Slayer was up to, we don't want to scare him off before we have the opportunity to speak to him."

We were quiet as the waitress brought our food. It really did look delicious and I really was hungry. The soup was thick and creamy, with a cheesy flavor that wasn't overwhelming, the broccoli chopped fine, and there was evidence of diced potatoes and carrots as well. The sandwich was piled high with freshly carved turkey, and the bread appeared to be homemade.

"Given the joint's somewhat shabby condition, I wasn't expecting a whole lot, but the food is excellent," I whispered.

Jack took a bite of his sandwich. "I guess this is a typical case of not judging a book by its cover."

"I know people say that, but I have to admit I almost always choose books based on my attraction to the cover."

Jack smiled. "Yeah, I do too. My first publisher and I had a huge argument about the cover for my second novel. He wanted something really modern-looking, with bold lettering and an almost futuristic image, while I wanted something warm yet somewhat out of focus to draw the reader in yet leave them wondering. I won the argument, or I suppose I should say my mother acting as my agent did."

"And how did the book sell?"

"It was on the best-seller lists for months."

We continued to talk about books we'd read and movies we'd seen while enjoying our lunch. Then we headed out to the SUV, and Jack scraped the snow from the windshield before we drove to the police station. It had been my experience that small-town cops—or most cops in general, really—were either very helpful or extremely closemouthed. I hoped whoever was on duty would be the former.

"Can I help you?" the young officer at the counter asked.

Jack introduced himself, taking the time to play up the newspaper-owner angle. He then introduced me before pushing the photos of Emily and Slayer toward him. "We're looking for the woman in this photo. She's the sister of a friend of ours and has been missing since last May. We believe she may have been in Fort Collins the March before that with the man in the other photo. He calls himself Slayer, but I understand his real name is Myron Black. We were hoping someone in town, perhaps one of your officers, had seen them."

He looked at the photo and frowned. Then he looked at Jack before taking a step away from the counter. "I'm going to have to ask you to come in to the conference room." He walked around to open the half door that separated the lobby from the bull pen. "Please. Come with me."

I glanced at Jack, who shrugged before taking my hand and following the officer through the half door, down a narrow hallway, and into a room with a long table surrounded by chairs. "Have a seat. I'll have someone come in and speak to you shortly." The officer left us, closing the door behind him.

"What do you suppose this is all about?" I asked.

Jack's eyes narrowed. "I'm not sure, but it looks as if there may be more going on than we first suspected."

I sat back in my chair and let out a breath. "Yeah. That definitely wasn't the response I was expecting. It's almost as if the officer went from boredom to suspicion in a few seconds. I wonder if Slayer's wanted for something. Maybe they think we know something about where Slayer is, or at least why he was here in March."

"I guess we'll find out soon enough."

It was just like Jack not to freak out even when the situation clearly called for at least a minor meltdown. I realize I'd just been thinking earlier that his easygoing approach to life was to be admired, but there were times when a small showing of anxiety would not only be understandable but, in many ways, warranted.

Jack must have picked up on my distress because he laced his fingers through mine. I don't know why I was so nervous. All the officer had done was indicate he wanted to discuss things further. Wasn't that what we wanted? So why did I feel like a caged animal in the small, windowless room?

"Mr. Jackson, Ms. Hanford," a tall middle-aged man with hollow cheeks and eyes so dark they appeared black, walked through the door the young officer had just closed. "My name is Officer Grant. I understand you're here to inquire about the individuals in these photos." He held up the photos we'd brought with us.

"That's correct," Jack answered. "The woman is Emily Halliwell. She's the sister of a friend of ours, Nicole Carrington. Emily left home last March and was communicating with Nicole until this past May. Nicole hasn't heard from her in almost nine months and is understandably worried. We're trying to locate Ms. Halliwell by backtracking to places it's believed she's been. The man in the other photo is believed to have been with her. His name is Myron Black, although he calls himself Slayer. We're hoping one of you might have some insight into why they were in Fort Collins or where they were planning to go from here."

"So, you haven't personally seen either of these individuals?"

Jack shook his head. "We only just heard of them a few days ago."

"Yet you came all the way from…" Officer Grant let the sentence dangle.

"Gull Island, South Carolina," Jack responded.

"That's quite a long way to come to gain information about someone you've never met and didn't even know existed a week ago."

"Is there some sort of a problem?" I asked. "It almost sounds as if you suspect us of something."

"You said the woman who asked you to track down her sister is named Nicole Carrington?" the officer asked.

"Yes, that's right," I answered.

"And how well do you know this Ms. Carrington?"

I could feel myself beginning to squirm. "Not all that well. She rents a cabin at the writers' retreat I run."

"Writers' retreat?"

I took a moment to describe the retreat, the people who lived there, and the meetings we had each week.

"So, you met this woman in November. She moved into one of your cabins to look for her sister, but never mentioned that to you until earlier this week. You have a resort to manage, and you," he gestured to Jack, "have a newspaper to run, yet you jumped on a plane and headed north during a snowstorm to try to track down a teenager who has supposedly been missing for going on nine months?"

Everything he'd said was true, but the way he'd said it made me feel like I needed to defend the actions Jack and I had taken.

Before I could speak, Jack asked, "Is there a reason you're asking us these questions?"

The officer didn't respond.

"Have you or have you not seen the people in these photos?" Jack snapped. It was obvious his take-it-as-it-comes approach to life had been stretched to the limit.

Officer Grant nodded. "I believe I may have seen the man in the photo."

Jack let out a breath. "Now we're getting somewhere. Do you have any idea why he was here or where we might find him now?"

"If my suspicion is correct, I do know where he is."

"Where?" I sat forward. I figured if we found Slayer, we'd find Emily.

"In the local cemetery."

My heart sank. "The cemetery? He's dead?" I could barely recognize the high, squeaky voice that asked the question as belonging to me.

"I believe so. I'll need to run some tests, but it seems your missing person might be my John Doe."

Chapter 7

"John Doe?" I continued to screech.

Grant nodded. "In March of last year, we discovered the body of a male who'd died from a bullet to the chest. He'd been moved from the crime scene and dumped in the forest just outside town. He wasn't carrying any identification and his prints weren't in the system. We tried for several months to identify him but were unsuccessful, so we took tissue and blood samples, cremated him, and buried him in the town cemetery. Based on the photo you have, I'm willing to bet that the man in the photo and the man in the cemetery are one and the same."

"If you cremated and buried him, can you even prove the gunshot victim in your cemetery is Myron Black?" I asked.

"As I said, we took samples as well as photographs. I also have the coroner's report. Now that I have a name, I'll track down medical and dental records and match them with the information we logged. It'll take some time to make a positive ID, but the tattoos displayed by the man in the photo match our John Doe. I think we can say with a pretty significant degree of certainty this is the same man."

I glanced at Jack. "If Slayer died in March, who was Emily traveling south with?"

Jack's brows were furrowed, leaving a deep line in the center of his forehead. "I have no idea."

After Officer Grant allowed us to leave, Jack and I returned to our motel room to regroup. The fact that Slayer had most likely been dead since before Emily even began her trip south left us with a whole lot of questions. Who had killed Slayer, and why? The murder remained unsolved. Had Emily come to Fort Collins with Slayer? Had she been here when he was murdered, or had she been waiting for him somewhere else, become tired, and set off on her own?

"What now?" I asked Jack after we'd discarded our outerwear and taken seats at the little table in the corner of the room.

"I'm not sure. Our primary objective has always been to find Emily. If she never came north with Slayer but instead found another traveling companion for the journey south, looking in to Slayer's death would be a waste of our time. On the other hand, if her new traveling companion is in some way related to Slayer's death, finding out what happened here last March could very well be the information we need."

I bit my bottom lip. "We have the selfies Emily sent Nicole. The one taken on March 20 hasn't been identified. That was the first one Emily sent, so if she was in Fort Collins with Slayer, it makes sense it could have been taken here."

"So we should walk around town to see if we can match it up."

"That would be my suggestion."

I set the photo on the table between us. A smiling Emily stood in front of a gray pillar that looked as if it were made of rock or mortar. It was a close-up of Emily's face, so there wasn't a lot of background, but it appeared as if there was snow behind the pillar. To the left was a strip of black. From what I could see, the pillar was either placed next to, or in front of, a black sign or wall.

Jack picked up the photo to take a closer look. "It's not a lot to go on."

"No, it isn't. But we came all the way up here, so we may as well take a walk around town. Maybe we can identify the location, and while we're looking, we can ask around about Emily and Slayer. If even one person saw them together, we'll know she was here."

I glanced out the window. The snow seemed to be increasing in intensity. "We should go now; the storm is only getting worse as the day progresses. Any idea where to start?"

Jack looked out too. "Maybe we should take a drive around. Familiarize ourselves with the lay of the land. Maybe we'll even find those pillars."

Fort Collins was a small town, so it didn't take long to explore the commercial center. Most of the structures were made of wood or red brick, and we didn't find evidence of pillars made of rock or mortar with anything black with a smooth surface next to them. After we had done what we could by driving aimlessly around, we parked.

"Afternoon. Can I help you?" a short, stocky woman who seemed as wide as she was tall asked from behind the counter of the first small store we entered.

"I hope so," I said as I navigated my way through scented candles, lotions, and oil pots. "My name is Jill Hanford, and this is Jack Jones. We're looking for this woman." I handed the photo of Emily to her. "She would have been in town last March. I know that was a long time ago, but I hoped you might have remembered seeing her."

The woman took the photo, pausing for a moment to study it. Eventually, she shook her head. "No. She doesn't look familiar." She handed me back the photo. "I'm sorry. It doesn't look as if I can help you."

"How about this man?" Jack handed the woman the photo of Slasher. "Does he look familiar?"

She grimaced. "That's John Doe. There was a drawing of him in the local newspaper last spring. I don't think they ever did find out who he was. Seems they buried him in the local cemetery."

"Other than seeing the sketch in the newspaper, do you remember seeing him when he was alive?" Jack asked. "Maybe walking around town or eating in a local diner?"

The woman shook her head. "No. I'm afraid I can't help you there either. If I'd seen him, I'd have remembered."

We thanked her for her time and went on from shop to shop. Each shop owner or employee said much the same thing as the first; no one remembered seeing Emily and everyone remembered seeing the sketch of Slayer in the newspaper, but no one had seen him in person. We'd been trudging through the snow for over two hours when we caught our first break.

"I don't remember the woman, but I know where she's standing."

"Where?" I asked a tall, thin blonde who owned what appeared to be the only dress and formal wear store in town.

"The America's First Mile Marker."

"Can you give us directions to it?" I asked.

"Sure. It isn't far."

She wrote down directions, and we made our way back to the SUV. It was a short and fruitful drive. We compared the photo to the sign announcing America's First Mile and saw the shape, color, and what appeared to be the material of the object behind Emily matched the sign exactly.

"So, we know Emily was here," I said, "and Slayer died here. I think we can assume that while Emily might have arrived with Slayer, she left with someone else. What do we do now?"

Jack took my hand in his. "I'm not sure. My feet are so cold I can't feel them anymore. Let's go back to that little bar we stopped in a while back. We can have a drink, warm up, and talk about what to do next."

The place Jack referred to was named, appropriately, The Border Bar and Grill. Now my entire body was frozen, so I chose an Irish Coffee, extra coffee, while Jack went with a beer on draft. The bartender who'd been working when we'd been there earlier was gone, and in his place was a much younger man with a mop of long black hair, an eyebrow ring, and a colorful tattoo of a python around his neck.

"What brings you folks to town?" the man, who introduced himself as Larry, asked.

"We're looking for these two." Jack slid the photos across the bar. "Have you seen them?"

"I've seen him." Larry pointed to the photo of Slayer. "He was a friend of Wader. According to the local paper, he's dead now."

"Did you ever speak to him?" Jack asked.

"No. Wader lives west of here, on a patch of land that can be accessed by dirt road during the summer and snowmobile during the winter. He's not particularly sociable, doesn't come into town more often then he needs to, but I remember him coming into the bar a while back. Must have been about a year ago. He had this man with him, but I was busy that night and Wanda was waiting tables, so I never spoke to either of them. Next thing I knew, the guy's sketch was in the paper and the cops were looking for anyone with information about his body."

"Did you tell the police you'd seen John Doe with Wader?"

He shook his head. "I mind my own business. It's the best way to stay out of trouble. You want a refill on that beer?"

Jack shook his head.

"And you don't remember seeing the woman in this photo? We believe she may have been traveling with the man you saw with Wader," I prodded.

"She doesn't look familiar."

"Can you tell us how to contact Wader?" Jack asked.

"He doesn't have a phone. If you want to talk to him, you'll need to sled out to his place, but I wouldn't recommend it. Wader is just as likely to shoot you for trespassing as he is to invite you in and answer your questions."

"We'll take that into consideration. I don't suppose you could draw us a map to his place?"

Larry looked as if he was going to refuse until Jack pulled out his wallet and began counting out twenty-dollar bills. When there were at least fifteen of them piled up, he grunted, grabbed a napkin, and began drawing. "This will get you out to Wader's place, but like I said, I wouldn't recommend going out there without an invite."

"And how would someone go about getting an invitation?" I asked.

Larry shrugged. "Guess you'd need to wait and run into him in town."

"And how often does he come into town?"

"Like I said, not often."

I glanced at Jack. He shrugged.

"Thank you for the map," Jack said. "If we decide to make the trip, do you know where we can rent snowmobiles?"

"If you're fool enough to go out to Wader's, you can rent the machines from the filling station on the far-west side of town. It'll take about an hour to get from the filling station to Wader's place, and I definitely wouldn't do it after dark."

Jack held his hand out to shake hands with Larry, who simply ignored it. "Thank you for your help. If you remember anything else about either of these people, we're staying at the motel south of town."

We left the bar and went to the motel to regroup. We'd planned to leave early the next morning to make our way back to Bangor in time for our late-afternoon flight. It was late in the day now, much too late to pay a visit to Wader. If we decided it was important to do so—and in my mind that was a big if, given the risk—we'd need to change our flights.

In the end, we decided to change our flight from Bangor back to Charleston via LaGuardia from Saturday to Monday. That would give us enough time, we reasoned, to finish looking in to things here in Fort Collins.

After changing the reservations, Jack went to the motel office to inquire about staying two extra nights. The place was only about half full, so we didn't think it was going to be a problem. I suggested that he ask the desk clerk for a recommendation for dinner while he was at it. The food at the diner where we'd had lunch was good, but it would be nice to have the final meal of the day in a place with better atmosphere.

Jack came back to the room to tell me things were set for the two extra nights. The desk clerk had told him about a lodge outside of town that catered to hunters and fishermen during the summer and fall but had an excellent restaurant year-round. Jack called to make a reservation we probably didn't need, and I went into the bathroom to take a quick shower.

******

The lodge was built from roughly hewn logs that perfectly matched the rugged landscape. As promised, the restaurant was lovely, with wooden tables and heavy chairs set around a large rock fireplace dominated the room. I could have done without the animal heads on the walls, but otherwise the place felt exactly right.

Jack was brave and ordered the moose steak, but I stuck with the lobster, which I'd been assured had been flown in fresh that day. The restaurant was probably half full, but I could picture it filled to the brim with sportsmen gathered here at the end of the day to talk about their conquests and share colorful tales of their time in the wilderness.

"How's your steak?" I asked after our entrees had been served.

"Really good. And the lobster?"

"Good as well. Actually, the whole meal has been excellent." I glanced around the room at the other patrons, who were likewise enjoying themselves. "Have you noticed, the man sitting alone at the table in the corner keeps looking at us."

Jack turned his head slightly and considered the man I'd indicated. "I don't know that he's looking at us specifically as much as he's alone and scanning the room, probably to entertain himself."

"No, I don't think so. I get the distinct impression he's watching us. He has a book he's pretending to read, but every minute or so he looks up, looks directly at us, and then looks down again, but he hasn't turned a page since we've been here."

Jack smiled. "Maybe he isn't watching us so much as you're watching him. He may have picked up on that, so he keeps looking up to see if you're still looking in his direction."

Jack might have a point. He'd caught my eye when he'd first come in, and I suppose I'd spent an inordinate amount of time looking in his direction. I made a concerted effort to look back at my food and my companion and to ignore the man I couldn't seem to stop staring at.

"What time do you think we should head out in the morning?" I asked Jack.

"Larry from the bar said it would take about an hour to get out to Wader's by snowmobile. I called the filling station and reserved two. Have you ever driven a snowmobile?"

"Never."

"Then we'll want to take it slow, just to be safe. The man I spoke to told me Wader kept a trail worn down, and a few other people live in the same direction who used it as well, so he didn't think we'd have a hard time navigating our way."

"Did he, like Larry, warn you that just showing up at Wader's unannounced was a bad idea?"

"He did. But he added that as long as we bring a gift for our host, we aren't likely to be shot."

"A gift?"

"He recommended cigarettes and whiskey, both of which he can sell me when we arrive to pick up the sleds. I told him we'd be by at around ten. I figured we should allow five hours for the round trip, just in case. The warmest part of the day is between ten and three. That will also give us time for a hearty breakfast; we're unlikely to get a chance to eat lunch."

The thought of taking off into the wilderness on a snowmobile had my stomach churning just a bit. I think the idea of happening across the wildlife that lived in the area had me more nervous than the unwelcome greeting we'd already been told to expect from Wader. I'm not a wildlife expert, but I was pretty sure bears would still be hibernating, but that didn't mean there weren't other large animals who might be equally likely to take a bite out of you lurking about.

"Wait a minute before you start the car," I said to Jack after we'd finished eating, paid the bill, and come out to the parking lot where we'd left the SUV.

"Why?"

"I just want to see if the man who was watching us leaves now that we have."

"You know, if we sit out here without starting the car and turning on the heater, we'll freeze to death."

"Two minutes. Just wait two minutes."

Jack shrugged. "Okay. If it will make you happy." He opened the door and I climbed inside, while Jack scraped the windows. Once they were clear, he climbed inside and joined me. After just a minute, the man came out of the lodge, climbed into a truck, and drove away.

"Ha. I told you he was watching us."

"Just because he left shortly after we did doesn't mean he was watching us. He arrived at about the same time we did, so it makes sense he would finish at about the same time."

"We didn't stay for dessert," I pointed out.

"He might not have either." Jack started the engine. "I'm sure the fact that we arrived and left at the same time is just a coincidence." He clicked on the heater.

"Maybe," I said as Jack pulled onto the highway. "But I'm going to keep my eyes and ears open for the next two days. Someone killed Slayer, and that someone might still be in town. If they are, they may not take kindly to the fact that we're here stirring things up."

Back at the motel, Jack opened the door to our room and motioned for me to precede him.

The first thing I noticed was that our suitcases had been opened and the contents had been dumped on the bed. The second was that the file of notes and photos Nicole had given us was gone.

Chapter 8

Saturday, February 3

Jack and I stuck to our plan to show up at the snowmobile rental place the following morning at ten, despite the break-in. We weren't sure who'd done it, but there hadn't been any evidence of forced entry, so my money was on the desk clerk, who not only had a key but had helped Jack make the dinner reservation, so knew we'd be gone and for about how long. I didn't know why he would rob us, but no other guests admitted to having seen or heard anything, which indicated to me that whoever entered the room was able to slip in and out without raising suspicion. Luckily, Jack had extra photos of Emily and Slayer in the truck, and for some reason his laptop hadn't been taken or tampered with.

Jack filled out the required paperwork and paid for a full day's rental, and I followed him on my snowmobile as he slowly made his way through the dense forest toward Wader's property. I knew the trip would take about ninety minutes given the speed at which we were traveling, so I let my mind wander. I'd called the resort earlier to check in with whoever was around to answer the landline at the house. As it turned out, it was George I spoke to. He'd popped over to build the fires and help Vikki with the puppy and kids. He'd taken Kizzy out while Clara made pancakes, Vikki had made sure the girls were ready for school, and Brit had seen to the twins. By my calculations, it had taken four adults to see to the needs of four children and a puppy. As a single mom, how was Abby ever going to manage? I supposed single parents across the globe figured it out, but from where I was sitting, the whole thing seemed like a huge undertaking for one woman to handle. Perhaps when this investigation was over, I'd bring up the subject of a full-time nanny for Abby once the baby was born.

After almost an hour, Jack stopped his machine, slipped off his helmet, and turned around. "You doing okay?"

I nodded. I didn't want to have to take my helmet, complete with face shield, off only to have to put it back on again, so I skipped a verbal reply.

"We should be more than halfway there. Once we see the fencing we were warned about, we'll stop before we approach the house."

Again, I nodded.

Jack turned back around, slipped his helmet over his head, and continued slowly.

I was glad Jack was taking his time. For one thing, I wasn't all that motivated to arrive at our destination, where we might very well be greeted with bullets aimed in our direction, but driving the snowmobile took some getting used to, so I was glad Jack hadn't decided to travel at a speed I wasn't comfortable with.

As we rode, I continued to let my mind drift. While surfing the web the previous evening, Jack had learned that Slayer's body had been found the day after Emily had sent her first selfie to Nicole. That seemed to fit the timeline until Jack read further and saw that the medical examiner had estimated the unidentified victim had been dead for two days prior to being found. That meant Slayer most likely was dead before the photo was sent. I wondered if Emily knew Slayer was dead and simply had done as Nicole asked, or if she'd hidden herself away somewhere waiting for Slayer to return, not yet aware he'd been shot.

The most disturbing thing Jack had found, in my opinion, was an article about a second body found on the same day as Slayer's, though there were differences between the two deaths. While Slayer had been found in the forest, the second body was left on the bed of an hourly motel west of town. And while Slayer was male and had been shot, the second victim was female and had been strangled. On the surface, the two victims and two crime scenes were about as different as they could be, yet two murders found on the same day in such proximity seemed suspect to us.

We arrived at the barbed-wire fence we'd been told served as a boundary of sorts for Wader's property. Jack pulled over, took off his helmet, and turned off his machine and I did the same, although it occurred to me that keeping the helmet on might not be a bad idea. Jack took the large paper bag filled with whiskey and cigarettes out of his backpack. He gave me a smile of encouragement, then took my hand with his free one, and slowly began to lead me toward what I was certain would be my untimely death.

My palms began to sweat despite the cold and my heart rate quickened as the shabby house came into view. There were several outbuildings in addition to the house, which I assumed served as a shed, a barn, and maybe a garage. There was smoke circling out of the chimney at the top of the house, demolishing my secret hope that Wader wasn't at home and we'd be able to skip the altercation completely.

We were perhaps twenty yards from the front porch when a large black dog came at us from out of nowhere. I instinctively froze. Jack did the same. While the dog stopped short of attacking us, he stood close enough for me to feel his warm breath as he growled in a very menacing manner. My gaze locked on the dog's huge teeth as we waited for Wader to come out and call him off. If he even intended to call him off. For all I knew, he would instead command the huge beast to tear into the uninvited visitors as an example to others who might dare venture onto his property.

"Good dog," I whispered in what I hoped was a soothing tone of voice as a man with a rifle finally emerged through the sagging front door. When I saw his cold stare, I wasn't sure whether to be relieved or even more terrified.

The man raised the rifle he carried and pointed it at Jack's chest. "Who are you and why are you trespassing on my property?"

Jack answered in a calm, confident voice. "My name is Jack. This is my friend, Jill. We're in the area to try to find a friend of ours. Her name is Emily. I spoke to Larry from the bar in town, who told me that you'd met with a man named Slayer last spring. The last we knew, our friend was traveling with Slayer. We'd like to ask you a couple of questions if you have a few minutes."

Wader didn't speak or call off his dog, but he didn't shoot us either. I guessed that was something.

"I brought whiskey and cigarettes." Jack held up his bag.

"Could use a drink." Wader lowered his gun. "Relax, Rufus."

The dog stopped growling and took a step back. I let out the breath I'd been holding.

"You can come in. For a minute," Wader specified.

Jack took a slow step forward. When Rufus didn't bite him, I followed slowly behind. By the time we made it to the front door, the dog, who had to weigh in at two hundred pounds, was wagging his tail.

"Nice place," Jack said as we entered the shabby room that seemed functional, if not homey.

"Whatever. Hand over the bag."

Jack did so, and Wader looked inside. I guess he was satisfied with what he saw. Without inviting us further into the room, he said we had two minutes, then asked what we wanted. Jack showed him Emily's photo, then explained who she was and why we were looking for her. He also gave a brief description of what we believed her relationship to Slayer might have been. Then Jack asked Wader if he'd be willing to share what he knew about either of them.

"Don't know the girl, but I knew Slayer. He had business in the area sometimes. And I had a cold one with him in town when he was here last year."

"Did Slayer ever mention the girl?" Jack asked.

"Not by name. Slayer did say there was a leech hanging on him that he'd finally managed to shake off."

My heart sank. "Shake off?" I asked.

Wader opened the bottle of whiskey and took a swig. "Seems like he met this girl south of here, and she decided the two of them should be a couple. Slayer was more of a love-'em-and-leave-'em kind of guy, wasn't looking for a permanent arrangement, but I guess the girl was persistent, so he let her tag along. Of course, once he got her here, he regretted it. Slayer wasn't one to spend a lot of time discussing his bedmates, but it sounded to me like she was a real pain in the backside, complained she was cold and wanted to go south. That's a dame for ya. They want a piece of your action, you decide to give it to them, and then they nag you from that day forward."

I circled back to the statement I was most interested in. "You said he shook her off. What did you mean by that?"

Wader took another long draw of the whiskey. At the rate he was going, he was going to finish the whole bottle in one sitting.

"Slayer said he and the girl had a fight and she stormed out. She was gone for a while, and when she came back to the room where they were staying it was to get her stuff. She told him she'd met someone who was heading south and was willing to take her along.

Slayer was more than done with her, so he wished her well and sent her on her way."

"Do you remember when that happened?" I asked.

"I guess a couple of days before Slayer went and got himself eliminated."

Emily had sent the photo to Nicole on Monday and Slayer had most likely died on Sunday, so she must have taken the photo prior to leaving Fort Collins but waited to send it when Monday rolled around. Knowing when she took the photos and when she sent them didn't necessarily coordinate was going to make it a lot harder to pin her down.

"Seems like your two minutes are about up," Wader said as he opened the door to show us out.

"Before we go, do you have any idea who killed Slayer?" Jack asked.

"Seems like I've already answered the number of questions the contents of this bag will buy you."

"I have money. I can pay you for additional answers," Jack offered.

He took out his wallet, which was still fat with twenties. During this trip, I had seen him take out his wallet on numerous occasions. I'd also seen him nearly clean it out more than once. He must be refilling it. We hadn't gone to a bank, so I wondered where he stashed his extra cash.

Jack handed Wader a wad of cash. Wader took a minute to count it.

"Okay," Wader eventually said. "You have two more minutes."

"Do you know who shot Slayer?" Jack asked.

"A guy named Falcon. Works the drug trade around here. Slayer figured he could worm his way in. He was wrong."

"Did you tell anyone, say the police, that you knew who their John Doe was and who'd shot him?"

"Nope."

That was a straight-enough answer.

"Do you know where this Falcon can be found?" Jack asked.

"Here and there. If I were you, I wouldn't go looking for him."

"And you know for a fact Falcon was the one who shot Slayer?" I clarified.

"Seen it with my own eyes. Now, I have some drinking to do, so we're done here."

The trip back to town was faster than the one out. For one thing, I had improved my driving skills. For another, I was a lot more motivated to get back to the motel room than I'd been to get to Wader's in the first place. Even with the faster pace, by the time we dropped off the snowmobiles, filled Officer Grant in on our conversation with Wader, and got back to our room, which looked just a bit dingier every time I saw it, it was late into the afternoon.

"Again, I have to ask, what now?" I flopped back on the bed and dropped my arm over my eyes. God, I was tired.

Jack sat down on the bed next to me. "I'm not sure. We aren't any closer to tracking Emily down or learning who was her traveling companion than we were when we first got here, but we've helped the police identify Slayer and given them a good lead on who his killer might have been. I feel like we've done all we can. But I've already changed our plane tickets to Monday, so we have a day to kill. We can either stay here and try to figure out who Emily left town with, or we can head back to Bangor tomorrow and take another look around there."

"My head is killing me after what seemed like hours on those machines. Let's get something to eat, then get a good night's sleep. We can decide what to do in the morning."

Chapter 9

Sunday, February 4

Officer Grant called us at the motel early the next morning, making our decision for us. He said he needed to ask us some follow-up questions and wondered if we could come by the station at around ten. Jack assured him that we'd be happy to help in any way we could, so we got dressed and got some breakfast. By the time we arrived at the police station, my head was swimming with questions, suppositions, and fears.

"Have a seat," Officer Grant said after he'd shown us into the same office where we'd been interviewed before.

"Does this have to do with Slayer's murder?" I asked. Jack and I had agreed to let the officer run the show and only answer questions as they were presented to us, but I was a bundle of nerves and the question came spilling out.

"Not exactly. We've verified the body buried in the local cemetery under the name John Doe is indeed that of Myron Black and have contacted his next of kin. We're arranging to have the remains delivered to his family. We've also contacted the state police regarding the involvement of the man known as Falcon in his death. Certain facts we've been able to dig up do seem to line up with the idea that Falcon is the killer. We've interviewed Wader in some depth. He wasn't thrilled to be involved but is cooperating. The reason we called you in today is to ask some additional questions regarding Emily Halliwell's disappearance."

"Okay," I said. "What do you want to know?"

"You said she spoke to her sister on March 11, at which time she agreed to send her a selfie once a week."

I nodded. "That's correct."

"According to the file the sister provided to you, she received the first photo on March 20. You've since confirmed that the photo was taken in front of the First Mile sign near the border."

"That's also correct," I said.

"When we spoke yesterday, you said that according to Wader, Emily—or at least the girl who had been following Myron Black around—had left Fort Collins with someone else. A man heading south."

I confirmed that everything Officer Grant had said to that point was correct based on what we'd been told by others.

"You also came to the conclusion, from what Wader told you, that Emily may have taken the photo earlier in the week only to wait to send it to her sister on Monday."

I nodded. "Wader made it sound as if Emily left Fort Collins before Slayer died. According to what you told us, it sounded as if Slayer died on Sunday, the day before Emily sent the first photo to her sister." I tilted my head slightly. "Is there a reason we're going over all this again?"

"There is. It didn't occur to me until after we spoke yesterday that Emily's route south, based on the photos she sent her sister, mimicked, in part, another route of interest."

"Okay," I said. "Go ahead."

"As you know, a second body was found the same day as Myron Black's. The second victim was a local prostitute who was found strangled in an hourly motel west of town. Her body was found on Tuesday and it was assumed she'd been killed on Monday night. We let them continue to assume that because it served our purposes, but the truth is, she had actually been dead for several days."

"Several days? And the motel staff didn't know they had a dead woman in one of their rooms?"

"The room was paid for by this man." Officer Grant pushed a sketch of a man with small eyes, a narrow face, and a heavy beard, across the table. "He paid cash for a week up-front. He left instructions that he wasn't to be disturbed for any reason and declined maid service. The week he'd paid for was up on Tuesday, which is when the maid found the body. The ME felt the body had been there since Friday or Saturday."

"Wouldn't the smell have alerted someone before then?" Jack asked.

"It should have, but it was March, with daily high temperatures below freezing. The room's back window had been left open and the heater had been turned off. Truth be told, the motel smells pretty bad even when there isn't a body to stink it up."

"What are you saying?" I asked. A feeling of dread had begun to build in my stomach.

"We believe the killer left town on Friday or Saturday after strangling his victim. It sounds as if the missing girl left town at the same time."

I was sure the color had drained from my face. "And you think they were together?"

"Not at first. But I did some checking, and now I'm not so sure they weren't traveling together."

"Checking?" I said weakly. "What kind of checking?"

"There were strangulation victims in other states in the weeks following the death of the local prostitute. On March 28, the body of a woman who worked as an escort was found in a seedy motel outside Salem, Massachusetts. Like this victim, she was strangled to death. On April 18, the body of a woman who worked in a strip club was found in another seedy motel on another highway outside of Atlantic City, New Jersey. She was also strangled."

Oh God.

Officer Grant continued. "After we spoke yesterday, I remembered your missing girl was moving south hugging the coast. I rechecked the dates and found that two of the selfies were sent to the sister from Salem on March 27 and Atlantic City on

April 17. Each the day before the two bodies were discovered."

I wanted to say something. I knew I should. But my mind was frozen in terror.

"So, you think Emily met and somehow hooked up with the person responsible for these deaths," Jack said.

"I think it's a theory worth exploring. So far, the murders have been investigated as isolated incidents. The idea that one person might have been responsible for all three deaths hasn't, as far as I know, been considered. To be honest, I wouldn't have made the connection myself if I didn't have a paper with the dates on which Emily sent photos to her sister sitting on my desk, staring me in the face. I'm still not certain we're looking at a serial killer, but I do think we have enough information to take a serious look at the possibility."

"How can we help?" Jack asked.

"Since we spoke yesterday, I've completed a thorough search for unsolved deaths by strangulation that involved women working in the sex industry in the past year. In addition to these three deaths, I found one in Newport, Rhode Island, on April 4 and another in Wrightsville Beach, North Carolina, on May 2. I'm going to need copies of all the photos sent by Emily to her sister."

"Someone was in our motel room while we were at dinner on Thursday," I said. "They took the file with all the photos, although Jack had copies. Do you think the killer knew we were snooping around and came looking for any evidence we might have?"

"Actually, no," Officer Grant replied. "My guess is the killer is long gone. I think it's more likely whoever was in your room is involved with the man who killed Myron Black, or it could have been a common thief looking for something of value." Officer Grant looked directly at Jack. "I understand you've been flashing a huge wad of cash around town. Not the best idea in these parts, or anywhere else, for that matter."

"Duly noted. I'll be more careful in the future."

"Back to Emily," I said. "What do we do now? How can we know for sure?"

Officer Grant's face softened a bit. "I know you're concerned for your friend's sister, but I don't think there's anything you can do right now. Even if I can prove one man killed all those women, and that man is the one in the sketch I have from the motel outside of town, it's been almost nine months since the girl's been heard from. If she was with him, she's probably dead."

We'd known from the beginning that it was likely Emily was dead even before a possible serial killer entered the scene, but it was still hard to hear someone say it so matter-of-factly. "Is there anything else you want to know?" I asked.

"Let's go over everything again," Officer Grant suggested. "We'll start with the initial phone call from Emily to her sister. We'll track her movements based on the photos and go over in detail what Emily's sister discovered at each stop. I want to know who she spoke to and what was said. The fact that the trail ends on Gull Island seems relevant. Not only did Emily stop sending photos, but I haven't found a single killing that meets the criteria I set up after May 7."

"May 7? There was a murder matching the others on Gull Island on May 7?"

"Gull Island, no. Charleston, yes."

******

Later that afternoon, I called Rick. I knew Officer Grant had spoken to him on the phone several times over the past twenty-four hours, and that he had filled Nicole in on what was going on because one of the telephone conversations between them had been a conference call that included her. This was now a multistate investigation, so the FBI had taken over. It looked like the disappearance of a supposed runaway teen was now being taken seriously.

"The feds believe the man they're looking for is an ex-con named Wayne Dillard," Rick began when I asked for an update. "He's thirty-eight-years-old and has several convictions for assault under his belt. The feds are circulating a photo of him to the owners and desk clerks at the motels where the bodies were found. There've been several witnesses who've confirmed that he's the man who paid cash to rent the rooms where the murder victims were found."

"What does that mean as far as finding Emily goes?" I asked.

"If Emily is alive and out there somewhere, this might actually help us. The feds have put out an all-points bulletin for both Dillard and Emily. They also have agents revisiting all the stops we know Emily made from the photos."

"I guess that's good," I said, although I was far from relieved.

"There's one more thing," Rick said. I heard the hesitation in his voice. "The feds are concerned because Jack owns a newspaper and you freelance for major news organizations. It's imperative that Dillard not know he's been identified or that the feds are on to him. Both of you need to keep a lid on this for now."

"Of course," I responded. "It never entered our minds to do otherwise, although now that you mention it, I suppose Jack and I have been handed a huge opportunity to be the first to report that a new serial killer has been identified."

"But you won't," Rick repeated.

I glanced at Jack. He shook his head. "No, Jack and I won't leak anything. When Dillard is captured and secrecy is no longer an issue, we'll be asking for an exclusive."

"I'll speak to the people I've been working with to let them know where you stand. Will you be home tomorrow?"

"Yes, but it'll be late."

"Okay. Perhaps we'll have news by then."

"I really hope so," I answered, even though there was still a pain in my stomach warning me that the news we were waiting for wasn't necessarily going to be good.

I hung up and looked at Jack. "I assume you picked up the gist of the conversation?"

"Man in the sketch has been identified, there's an APB out on both him and Emily, and the feds don't want the fact that they're on to him showing up in the news."

"That's about it." I leaned back in the chair I was sitting in and crossed my legs beneath my body. "You know, there was a time I would have been in favor of running the story no matter the consequences to the investigation or the lives affected. As a young reporter I hung my hat on the concept of the public's right to know. I guess I still believe that to an extent, but I've been around long enough to realize the press can muddy the water in an active police investigation. If the man from the sketch did kill all those women and may very well have killed Emily, I don't want to be the one to tip him off that the feds are on to him. The last thing we want is to give him time to flee."

Jack was sitting on the bed leaning against the pillows piled up between his back and the wall. "I agree. I love owning my little newspaper and writing about events in my little corner of the world, but I don't have the kill-or-be-killed instinct it takes to get in the middle of the type of articles that very well might change the world, or at least some aspect of it."

"Yeah."

"When you were working in the industry, did you ever print a story that ended up doing harm to anyone?" Jack asked.

I looked at the man I loved. I hated to tell him, but I also didn't want to lie. "I did. It was shortly after I was hired by my last employer. I fell into some information that provided delicate details about the investigation into a man who was wanted for the rape of five women. I knew the investigation was ongoing, and on some level I even suspected my printing the information I'd found thanks to nothing more than dumb luck could hinder the case the cops were building, but I wrote the story anyway. Writing that article, and including that information, helped send my career to the next level. It also resulted in the rape of three more women before the man was finally captured."

"That's rough."

"What's rough is the tongue-lashing I received from the lead investigator, who made sure I fully understood I was the one who was responsible for the rape of the last three women. He made sure I knew my story had foiled the plan the police had had to bring him in before those rapes occurred." I glanced at Jack. "He was right. It was my fault those women were forced to endure what they did."

"Someone else might have found the same information and run with it, leading to the same result."

Jack was trying to give me an out, to let me off the hook. "Maybe. But someone else didn't run the story. *I* did. After the guy left my apartment, I had a total meltdown. I thought about quitting journalism altogether, but I didn't. I have, though, been a whole lot more conscientious about what I run and who it might affect."

Jack got up, walked across the room, and sat down next to me. He took my hand in his. "Sometimes all we can do is learn from our mistakes. It sounds like you did. Perhaps it's time to stop beating yourself up over it."

I knew Jack was right, but I'd never forgive myself for allowing my ambition to cause harm to three women I didn't know and would never meet.

Chapter 10

Tuesday, February 6

The morning dawned drizzly and overcast. After the long day of travel on Monday, I was tempted to pull the covers over my head and sleep the morning away. I might have, had I not had obligations to see to. Abby had a doctor's appointment and Vikki was taking her, so I'd volunteered to keep an eye on the boys while they were away. The girls would be in school, so it would be just the three of us for an hour or so. I didn't have a lot of experience with three-year-olds, but I figured a Baggie full of Cheerios each and a cartoon marathon in the den would do the trick.

"Morning, everyone," I called as I walked into the kitchen. "Is that bacon I smell?"

"A bacon, egg, and cheese casserole," Clara answered, as I took a seat between George and Garrett after I'd poured myself a cup of coffee.

"Smells wonderful. I'll grab some after I wake up a bit. Where's Brit?"

"Taking the girls to school," Vikki said. "Abby and I will be leaving in about twenty minutes. Are you still good to keep an eye on the boys?"

"I've been planning on it."

"They want to do some extra tests today, so it may be a longer appointment than usual, but we should be back before noon. I'll text you when I have a better idea of how things are going," she added.

"So, what are you others doing today?" I said.

"Coincidentally, I have an appointment with the specialist I see occasionally in Charleston," Garrett answered. "George is driving me and Clara's coming along for the ride. I'm hoping I'll get the all-clear to start using a walker for short periods. I tire easily, but I've been doing better with my physical therapy and I'm pretty darn tired of sitting around in this wheelchair all day."

"It seems if you can get up they'd want you to," I replied.

"They just want to be sure the injuries I sustained from the fall when I had the stroke are healed up and my muscles have developed enough to hold my weight. They don't want me to reinjure myself, which they think I might if I try to use the walker without supervision. I've wanted to argue that the risk should be mine to take, but the physical therapy seems to be working, so I've pretty much decided to let the therapist set the pace."

I took a sip of my coffee. "I think that's smart."

"By the way, did Brit get the chance to chat with you after you got home last night?" Garrett asked.

"No. It was late, so I went straight up to my room. Did she need something?"

"She said she might have found a lead of some sort. Something to do with a photo-sharing file or service or something. I'll be the first to admit I'm a bit of a dinosaur when it comes to social media and internet sites. I know Brit had a few errands to do after she dropped the girls at school, but I imagine she'll be back before too long."

I stood up from my chair. "You know, everyone will be leaving soon, so I think I'll run upstairs and take a quick shower while I have the chance. If Brit does come back, let her know I'll be around all morning." I took several steps, paused, and turned back around. "What about Nicole? Has anyone seen her since the news of Emily's connection to the killer was shared with her?"

It seemed she'd left the resort yesterday morning and no one had seen her since. This wouldn't be the first time she took off for days at a time without a good-bye or an explanation, but the timing was unfortunate. If she wasn't in her cabin later, I'd try her cell. She shouldn't be alone to deal with this new complication, especially when there were so many of us close by who were willing to help her get through what were certain to be some very difficult days.

By the time I'd showered and dressed, Vikki had the twins bathed and dressed and sitting quietly in the den, watching talking dinosaurs on the television. Garrett was in his room, presumably getting ready for his doctor's appointment, but George and Clara were nowhere to be found. Vikki and Abby were in the kitchen making a grocery list. It made sense for them to stop off for the items we needed while they were out.

"You look rested," I said to Abby, who finally had some color in her cheeks after the ordeal she'd recently endured.

"Thanks. I feel rested. All Dr. Vikki here will let me do is eat and sleep."

"The baby needs to eat and sleep," Vikki corrected her with a smile.

"Well, thanks, no matter who you're looking out for." Abby turned to include me in her words. "All of you. I don't know what I would have done if you hadn't jumped in to help me when I needed it."

Vikki and I assured her we were happy to help, and the only thanks we needed would be the delivery of a healthy baby girl.

After Vikki and Abby left, I grabbed my laptop and joined the twins in the den. The first ten minutes were consumed with tales of the dinosaurs they were watching, but once they settled back into the action, I logged on and opened the file I'd been keeping about our search for Emily. I had no intention of publishing anything until I got the green light to do so, but eventually, the story of how the search for a runaway had led to the identification and arrest of a serial killer would be a good one. Of course, that was predicated on the fact that the man was found and apprehended.

I'd scanned all the photos pertinent to the case into my file, including the mug shot the feds had provided of Wayne Dillard. He wasn't a bad-looking man, without any of the attributes I'd suspect would be found on the face of a man who had brutally killed so many women. The sketch Officer Grant had first shown me made him look as if he had beady eyes and a narrow jaw, but the actual photo was of a man with a chin and eyes better proportioned to his face. I could see why someone like Emily, who was young and a bit reckless, would agree to travel with a man who looked so harmless. I wondered if she knew or even suspected he was killing women along the route after he'd dropped her off at whatever motel room or cabin he'd chosen for her. If she'd known, had she tried to escape?

I knew Rick had much more information than I did. We'd spoken briefly on the phone while we were laid over between legs of our trip the previous day, and he'd told me he was building a file that contained data not only on Wayne Dillard but on each of the murders that had been attributed to him. I couldn't imagine what might motivate a man to brutally murder women at a rate of almost one a week. Why had he started? Why had he stopped? Emily had hooked up with him at the location of the first murder in the spree, at least as far as anyone knew. Could she have done something to ignite the killing in the first place? Had she said something that set him off? Or had she simply been in the wrong place at the exact moment that some hidden psychosis waiting to see the light of day suddenly made itself known?

"Dinosaurs are over," one of the twins—I thought Tommy—informed me.

I glanced at the television. "Do you want me to change the channel or do you want to do something else?"

"We want Bob."

"Bob?" I had no idea who Bob was.

Tommy pointed to the TV. "He has a truck."

Okay, all I needed to do was find a cartoon featuring Bob with a truck. I decided the best tactic was to check the guide to see which cartoons were in this time slot.

"There's *Bob the Builder*," I said.

Tommy ran to the sofa and settled in next to his brother. I changed the channel and was relieved to see that Bob did indeed have a truck, as well as several other pieces of heavy equipment. I asked the twins if they wanted a snack, but they were fine. So I went back to the table and continued to work on my file.

Maybe after this show was over the boys would want to bundle up and take a walk. I was curious to see whether Nicole was back yet. Not that I'd want to have a conversation with her about her runaway sister or the killer she seemed to have been traveling with while the boys were within earshot, but I was somewhat concerned that she might become desperate enough to do something foolish. I know I'd certainly done a stupid thing or two in my time. For me, that seemed to be an auto response to extreme stress.

About halfway through *Bob the Builder*, Jack stopped by with Kizzy. Of course, once the boys saw the puppy, all thoughts of sitting quietly and watching TV were out the window. "I wasn't expecting you," I said after briefly greeting Kizzy, who had already gone on to the twins.

"I was out taking photos for the article I'm writing about the stockroom fire at the minimart, so I decided to stop by. Where is everyone?"

"Various appointments. I'm on twin duty this morning. I was thinking about taking a walk. Do you and Kizzy have time to come with us?"

"I'm sure Kizzy would like the opportunity to stretch her legs and I have some time. What time are the others supposed to be back?"

"Vikki and Abby should be back by noon, but Garrett, George, and Clara went into Charleston for the day. I planned to try to sit down with Rick to get more depth about the investigation when Vikki gets home to take over kid duty. I'm sure there will be new breakthroughs every day."

Jack helped me bundle the twins up in jackets and winter caps before going out into the chilly but not really frigid winter day. After spending a few days in northern Maine, our fifty-five-degree day seemed almost balmy.

"Was there a lot of damage at the minimart?" I asked Jack as we walked hand in hand along the trail leading to the cabins while Kizzy and the boys trotted in front of us.

"Enough to mandate closing until the repairs are made, but not enough for the repairs to take long. The owner assured me the minute the insurance adjuster gave him the go-ahead he'd make sure whatever needed to be done was taken care of as quickly as possible."

Kizzy dropped a stick at Tommy's feet, and he picked it up and ran with it instead of throwing it. Kizzy followed along behind without, fortunately, knocking him over.

"I'm going to run over to Nicole's to see if she's home. The others informed me that she'd been gone since she spoke with the police. Why don't you take Kizzy and the boys down to the beach? I'll meet you there in a few minutes."

"Okay. Take your time if she's home and needs to talk. We'll be just fine."

When I arrived at Nicole's, I could hear her talking. I wasn't sure if she had company or was on the phone. I considered walking away, but I really wanted to make sure she was all right, so I knocked. After a few seconds, Nicole answered the door. She looked surprised to see me but invited me in.

"I just wanted to be sure you were okay," I said lamely. "Which of course you aren't. Who would be? I guess I just wanted to see if there was anything I could do to help. I'm sure all this must be very difficult for you."

Nicole, who looked thin to the point of gauntness, nodded, indicating that I should take a seat. I sat down on the sofa and waited for her to join me. As soon as she sat down, she began to speak. "I am worried. Very worried. And I'm afraid I've done something stupid that has only made the situation worse."

Uh-oh. "And what did you do?"

Nicole handed me a flyer. It featured a photo of Emily with a notice offering a twenty-five-thousand-dollar reward to anyone who provided information leading to her whereabouts.

"My phone has been ringing nonstop with people calling to let me know they'd seen her. With the first couple of calls, I really hoped she'd been seen, but there have been so many sightings from one coast to the other that I've decided the leads are mostly useless. There's no way I can check them all out, and I'm beginning to doubt any of them are legitimate. The responses to my questions are much too vague to account for much."

"I'm sorry. I understand why you were motivated to do something to speed things up. I guess you could just turn off your phone."

"I've almost tossed the thing in the ocean more than once this morning." Nicole took a deep breath. "Is there any news? Actual news?"

I shook my head. "Not so far, but I'll keep you informed if I do find anything out."

"I'm just so scared."

I took Nicole's hand in mine. "I know. Me too." I glanced at the clock. "Jack and the twins are waiting for me at the beach. I can come back later if you want to talk. Just text me. And Nicole…"

"Yes?"

"If someone calls claiming to have information about Emily and they want to meet you in person to discuss it, don't go. Call me or Rick, but don't under any circumstances agree to meet any random person. There are a lot of wackos out there."

"You mean like the man my sister decided to take off with?"

"Exactly like that."

Chapter 11

Timmy and Tommy were ready for lunch and a nap after a long walk. Jack and I fed them and tucked them into bed, then settled at the kitchen table with a fresh pot of coffee. There were times I missed the snow of New York winters, but after surviving our trip to the blustery north, I was just as happy to be back to the milder temperatures of South Carolina in February.

"I just received a text from Vikki. She and Abby are on their way home. Brit is picking the girls up from school, so once Vikki gets here, I should be able to get away for the rest of the afternoon. I thought I'd text Rick to see if he's free to meet. I can make us some lunch, or we can stop at Gertie's on our way."

"Let's stop at Gertie's," Jack said. "I wanted to see if I could get a quote from her about the new food service tax the island council is considering."

"Food service tax?" I asked as I refilled my ceramic mug.

"I assumed you'd heard. It seems the council is trying to find new, innovative ways to get the visitors who come to the island to leave more money behind. A tax known as a TOT, or Transient Occupancy Tax, is already collected from visitors as part of their lodging fee. The property usually adds the fee to the sales tax, or it's sometimes charged separately as a resort tax. The council has been discussing a similar fee for meals served by full-service restaurants like Gertie's. It wouldn't apply to anything purchased from food trucks or drive-throughs."

I frowned. "That's sure to stir up some controversy."

"Oh, it already has. Which usually is bad for local morale but sells a lot of newspapers."

"And how does it make you feel to know your story will serve as a catalyst for conflict between friends and neighbors?" I asked in a teasing voice, although I was interested in the answer. I'd experienced similar correlations between bad news and increased sales when I worked in New York, which reminded me of the story I'd already told Jack.

Jack shrugged. "Someone has to stir the pot. I guess it might as well be me."

By one o'clock we were caught up on Abby's overall health, which was improving every day she was with us, and we'd filled Vikki in on the twins' nap, nourishment, and exercise needs. It was past the traditional lunch hour when we arrived at Gertie's, so the place was all but empty.

"What can I get you two?" Gertie asked after we'd taken stools at the counter.

"We're here for lunch," I replied. "What do you have on special?"

Gertie rattled off the soup and sandwich of the day, as well as the full-meal special, which today was pot roast with all the trimmings. We both ordered the soup and sandwich special, Gertie poured us cups of coffee, and Jack jumped in with his question about the tax.

"It's highway robbery, that's what it is." As predicted, Gertie's hackles were raised in a big way. "Folks gotta eat. Taxing food, whether you come by it at the market or my place, shouldn't even be on the table. You know what the problem is?" Gertie didn't wait for an answer. "The problem is greedy politicians trying to make a buck to pay for their pet projects."

"Can I quote you on that?" Jack asked.

"Damn right." Gertie launched into a drawn-out tirade that was sure to singe the ears of anyone in hearing range. I didn't like the tax myself, but I wouldn't want to be one of the island council members supporting it should Gertie attend an upcoming meeting, which she indicated she planned to do.

Jack and Gertie seemed to be enjoying volleying comments back and forth across some imaginary net represented by the tax, but it was giving me a headache. "So, talk to me about that new painting on the wall," I said to divert Gertie's attention now that Jack had his quote.

Gertie paused and looked at the large portrait of the wharf where Gertie's sat, along with the harbor and the colorful boats that were tied to buoys. "Quinten painted it." Quinten Davenport was a retired coroner and Gertie's current male companion.

"It's really good. Quinten certainly has real talent."

Gertie shrugged. "Said he needed something to occupy his time, so he decided to try his hand at painting. Told him my house needed painting, but he said that wasn't exactly what he had in mind."

"Well, the painting is lovely. Maybe I'll see if he's willing to do one of the resort. I'd love to capture one of the cabins with the sea or marsh in the background." I could just imagine a large painting on the wall of the foyer just as you entered the main house.

"Speaking of the resort, how's your search for Emily going?" Gertie asked. "I hoped I'd have heard she'd been found by now."

"I'm afraid things have become more complicated." I filled her in on the highlights, which had become increasingly more alarming with each passing day.

Gertie made a clicking sound with her tongue as she shook her head back and forth, as if trying to shake off an unpleasant thought. "I knew that girl was in some sort of trouble when she wandered in here that first day. I'm just sick to think something might have happened to that sweet little thing. What kind of a world are we living in where someone would do to another what that man did to them girls?"

"You said on the last day you saw Emily you offered her a job and a place to stay should she need it. Did she do or say anything that might indicate where she was heading, or what her long-term plans were?"

Gertie crossed her arms over her chest and leaned back so her hips were resting on the counter behind her. "I've been thinking about that a lot since that first time we spoke. I've asked myself time and again if the girl said anything that I might have missed, but there just wasn't anything." Gertie screwed up her lips. "Although…"

"Yes?" I asked.

"Emily did mention that one of our customers had offered her some clothes, hand-me-downs from her daughter, who was about the same size. The only reason she mentioned it was because I asked if she needed to do some laundry and she said she'd need to do some, but it could wait if the hand-me-downs worked out."

"Do you know which customer made the offer?" I asked.

Gertie tapped her finger to her chin. "Seems it must have been someone who was in on that last day." She paused and appeared to be pulling at a memory that was a bit too stubborn to make its own way to the surface. "I know Barbara Jean was in that day, but she only has sons. I remember Emily chatting with Brooke Johnson, but of course, it wouldn't have been her; her children are young'uns." Gertie paused another moment and then snapped her fingers. "Elvina Rayburn and Yvette Joplin were in for lunch that day. I remember Emily spent a few minutes chatting with them, and both women have daughters who graduated high school and headed for college last year. My money would be on one of them making the offer."

"Okay, we'll check with them," I said. "If Emily did go to meet with someone after she left here for the last time, it might help us put together a timeline. Do you remember what time she left here?"

"Three o'clock. Her shift was over at three o'clock."

Gertie went ahead and offered to call Elvina and Yvette for me while Jack and I were eating. Elvina hadn't been the one to offer the clothing; her daughter was a good six inches taller than Emily. She seemed to remember Yvette saying she had some clothes she planned to take to the secondhand store, but she didn't answer when Gertie called her, so she left my name and number and asked her to call me about the hand-me-downs.

Jack and I headed to the sheriff's office in the hope of seeing Rick. Now that the feds were in charge, we hoped we'd finally get the answers we were after.

"I'm afraid there isn't anything new," Rick said when we arrived. "The feds have issued the APBs for Wayne Dillard and Emily Halliwell, but as far as I know, they haven't heard anything. Of course, it isn't a given they'd tell me even if they had a new lead. All I can do is cooperate to the best of my ability and hope they keep me in the loop."

"Have you spoken to Nicole?" I asked.

"Not today. Why? Has she heard something?"

I handed Rick one of Nicole's flyers.

He cringed. "I wish she hadn't done that."

"I think she wishes the same thing. Her phone has been ringing off the hook with tips that Emily has been seen from one coast to the other. Even if she were to receive a legitimate one, she probably wouldn't recognize it as such unless she found a way to weed out the good from the bogus."

"Tell her to keep a low profile and not to answer any of the calls she receives. The feds aren't going to like that she's maneuvered herself into the middle of their investigation. Unfortunately, there's a good chance a local television station will latch on to the story if news of the flyers and reward gets out. If they do, there goes our element of surprise."

Rick wasn't wrong. Nicole had made a major mistake and the feds weren't going to be happy about it.

Jack launched into a conversation with Rick regarding the upcoming town council meeting while I excused myself to take a phone call from Yvette. I headed to the main lobby and looked out the large picture window as I spoke.

"Yes, I offered Emily some of the clothes my daughter Sissy decided she no longer wanted," Yvette said. "I could see they were about the same size and I just planned to donate them anyway."

"And did Emily come to get them?" I asked.

"She did, when she was off work for the day. I remember how excited she was to see things Sissy left behind were just the thing she'd enjoy wearing. She took her time and tried everything on. She told me that she didn't have a way to take everything with her, so she wanted to choose the things she felt best suited her."

"Did Emily do or say anything that might help us figure out what might have happened after she left your place? As far as we can figure out, you may have been the last person to see her. She didn't show up for work at Gertie's the following day."

As I waited for Yvette to reply, I glanced into the distance, where the peekaboo view of the harbor was masked by heavy clouds. We'd had more dreary days than sunny ones lately, and I was in the mood for a change of weather.

"You know, it did seem like she was nervous about something when she arrived. I pointed out that one of the blouses Sissy had left would be prefect for her to wear to work. She smiled and agreed, but I could see the happiness didn't reach her eyes. I offered her a snack after we'd sorted through the clothes, but she declined. And I asked if she was working the following day and she answered with something noncommittal. I think she said she hoped so but would need to see how things worked out." Yvette paused and then continued. "I remember going into the kitchen to find a grocery bag for Emily to carry the clothes she'd picked. When I came back she was staring at the television with an odd look on her face. No, not odd. I'd say the look was more terrified. I remember thinking all the color had drained from her face and she looked as if she might pass out. I asked her if anything was wrong and she said no. She thanked me for the clothes and left in a hurry."

"Do you remember what program was on the television?" I asked.

Yvette paused. "I don't recall exactly. I think it might have been one of those talk shows. Although it must have been around four-thirty by then, so I suppose it could have been a news show I watch sometimes from up north. My family is from Maine, so I sometimes tune into this show called *Northern Reports*. It's on channel twenty-eight at four-thirty before the local news."

"What sort of news items does the show feature?" I asked.

"All sorts of things. Weather, local events, police reports, even local politics."

The clouds that had blocked my view of the harbor suddenly cleared, allowing the sun to peek through for the first time since I'd been standing there. I had to wonder what Emily had seen on the television that day and whether whatever it was that had made her go pale was the same thing that made her disappear.

Chapter 12

The sun had just set when Rick showed up at the front door. I was about to invite him in when I noticed a black sedan with tinted windows and a second sheriff's vehicle behind Rick's in the drive.

"What's going on?" I asked as two men dressed in dark suits got out of the car.

"The federal agent in charge of the investigation wants to have a look around the grounds."

Behind the agents, I saw two men in sheriff's uniforms slipping leashes onto two German shepherds. "They think Emily is still on the grounds?" I said, my tone flat as it sank in that the animals I was watching were most likely cadaver dogs.

"It's a theory, given the information we have at this point," Rick answered. "It would be best if you, Nicole, and, well, everyone, waited in the main house until the team has completed their search of the property."

I nodded. "Everyone is here already except Alex and Nicole. Give me a minute. I'll call them and ask them to come over."

Rick took my hand in his and gave it a squeeze. "I'm sorry," he said, then walked away.

I took out my phone and called both Alex and Nicole. I didn't explain why I wanted them to come over, but I did say it was extremely important that they did. We'd had two other temporary residents, but one had moved out days afterward, claiming he couldn't think with all the quiet, and the other, a romance writer, was away at a writers' conference and wouldn't be back until next week.

Once Alex and Nicole arrived, I texted Rick to let him know the resort was clear and he and the team were free to do what they'd come for. Knowing what they were looking for and what they were likely to find had my stomach tied in knots.

"They think she's buried here at the resort," Nicole said in a tone that mimicked the emptiness I felt.

"It's a possibility they need to eliminate given the circumstances." I took Nicole's hand in mine. It was ice cold, despite the fact that the room was fairly warm. "We can't give up hope."

Nicole's large brown eyes looked like bottomless pools on her almost completely colorless face. "Why not?" Nicole whispered. "Will clinging to hope change the outcome of this whole thing?" Tears gathered at the corner of her eyes. "Is it more likely that they won't find a body if I cling to hope than if I give in to hopelessness and begin the grieving process now?"

"No," I admitted. "I guess not. If there's a body, they'll find it, and if there isn't, they won't. The outcome is set whichever way you choose to feel about it."

Nicole, who was now sitting at the dining table, crossed her arms over the tabletop, rested her head in her arms, and wept. I waited quietly with her there while the others retired to the living room to await the outcome. After a while, Nicole got up, dried her eyes, and began to pace. I sat quietly and continued to wait. I felt I should say something to ease the tension, but I had no idea what that would be.

"I should never have let her run off by herself," Nicole said in a quiet voice. She curled her fingers into her palms, creating tight fists that she tucked up under her armpits. "When she called and told me her plan, I should have done something. Something different. Something better."

"I'm not sure what you could have done," I answered softly.

Nicole glanced at me. Her eyes were cold. "I could have called the police, or I could have called my mother. I could have dropped everything and tried to track her down. I could have begged and pleaded with her. I could even have offered her money." Nicole nodded and went back to her pacing. "Yes, that's what I should have done. She would have come to me if I told her I had money for her trip. Once I had her with me, I could have found a way to make her stay." Nicole stopped walking and looked me in the eye. "If Emily is dead, it will have been my fault. I was an adult and she was a child. I should have done something, but I didn't." A single tear slid down her cheek. "Now I'll never get the chance."

I struggled for something to say, but words completely eluded me. I turned away from Nicole's intense stare. The photo of Emily standing in front of cabin six was on the table. To give myself something to do, I picked it up and pretended to study it.

"*Save the girl, save the girl*," Blackbeard said after flying into the kitchen and landing on the back of one of the dining chairs.

"Yes." I smiled at the colorful bird. "We're trying to save the girl."

Blackbeard cocked his head to the side, as if trying to make out what I was saying. "*Man bad, save the girl*."

I frowned. I'm not sure why it hadn't occurred to me before, but Blackbeard might have seen Emily when she was here. After Garrett had his stroke, he'd sent Rick to fetch Blackbeard and take him to the local veterinarian, who had agreed to keep him until Garrett was able to come home. When Rick had come to the house, he'd found the bird gone. He figured he must have gotten out when he and the other emergency personnel responded to Blackbeard's call that there was a "man overboard." Not knowing how to handle the situation and not wanting to worry Garrett, he'd told my brother Blackbeard was with the vet, then continued to look for him. He suspected he'd come home on his own, so he'd left the attic window open. Over the next few months, he'd kept looking for the bird, stopping off at the house every few days to see if he'd returned on his own. There was evidence Blackbeard had been coming back to the house, and there were a ton of sightings around the island, but until a friend of Garrett's came to stay at the resort to begin the renovations, no one had been able to capture him.

If Blackbeard was at the resort when Emily was here, he might very well be the only witness to what had happened to her.

"Did you see Emily when she was here?" I asked the bird.

"*Save the girl, save the girl.*"

"Yes, we're trying to save the girl. You said, 'man bad.' Did you see a man with the girl?"

"*Man bad, save the girl.*"

This was getting us nowhere. Blackbeard was able to communicate with an almost spooky degree of accuracy, but he had a limited vocabulary, so to understand what he was trying to tell you, you had to find words he could use to convey his message.

"You don't seriously think this bird saw what happened?" Nicole asked.

"He might have." I explained about Blackbeard being free to come and go while Garrett was in the hospital those first months, including during the time we knew Emily stayed here. "I know it's crazy to think he can communicate with people, but he's shown on numerous occasions that he's able to do just that."

"Parrots mimic; they don't communicate."

"I agree that in most cases parrots do simply mimic what they've heard, but Blackbeard is different. He's helped us solve mysteries in the past. He's special."

Nicole looked doubtful, but she didn't argue the matter.

"There you are, you sneaky bird." Garrett rolled into the kitchen. He looked at me. "I'm sorry. He was watching the movie with us and then flew away."

"It's okay," I assured Garrett. "I think he might have seen what happened to Emily. He keeps saying, 'man bad, save the girl.'"

Garrett looked at Blackbeard. "Did you see the girl?" He held up the photo. "Did you see Emily?"

"*Pretty girl, pretty girl.*"

"Yes." Garrett chuckled. "She is a pretty girl. Did you see what happened to her?"

"*Blow the man down, blow the man down.*"

"What does that mean?" Nicole asked. I could see the doubt that had been mirrored on her face had turned to curiosity.

Garrett turned his chair slightly so he was facing Nicole. "Blackbeard can have a lot to say, but he's limited to the words he's learned along the way. Blackbeard and I love watching pirate movies, and before I was in this dang chair, we liked playing pirate. I'd take him into town and he'd sit on my shoulder and talk to people we passed. It was really a hoot. But I digress. The point is that Blackbeard knows a lot of pirate sayings. 'Blow the man down' usually refers to a man being knocked down."

Nicole frowned. "Or a woman? Say if she were running from the man and fell?"

Garrett nodded. "Yes, I guess that could be the case."

Nicole threw her hands in the air. "I can't believe the only witness to my sister's death was a parrot." She lowered her arms. "Someone must have seen something."

Neither Garrett nor I answered. I was sure this waiting was killing her. I didn't know what to do, but I had to do something, so I crossed the room and began to make tea.

"If Blackbeard did see what happened to Emily, do you think he could show us where it was?" I asked Garrett.

"I'd think so. It's been a while, but Blackbeard seems to have a really good memory. It's dark now, but if the men don't find anything tonight, I suppose we can try having Blackbeard lead us to the scene of whatever he saw in the morning."

I was about to reply to Garrett's suggestion when I heard the dogs barking.

"They found her," Nicole said as she opened the back door and ran into the night.

I glanced at Garrett. "I'll get her. Tell the others to stay put until Rick says we can go out."

I grabbed my coat and headed out into the night. The cloud cover had returned, making it even darker than usual. I hadn't taken the time to grab a flashlight and couldn't see where Nicole had run off to, but I could hear the dogs barking and men yelling in the direction of the marsh, so I headed in that direction. When I got to the edge of the waterline, I found one uniformed man was holding both dogs back. Rick was hanging on to Nicole and the third deputy, Connolly, was wading into the marsh. Like the rest of the area, it was dark, but one of the FBI agents held a spotlight and was shining it into the inky darkness.

I froze as I watched the man wade deeper and deeper into the marsh, teeming with snakes, alligators, and other predators.

After a moment, I walked to Rick. "What is it? What did you find?"

"We aren't sure yet. The dogs are very interested in something in the water, so Connolly is checking it out."

I watched as the second man, the one who was holding the light, passed the light to the second FBI agent and was pulling on waders. The night was not only dark but eerily quiet. I felt a shiver run up my spine as I took another step closer to Rick.

Connelly stopped his forward progress. "I found something."

"Emily?" Nicole gasped.

"I don't know," he answered. "We'll need additional light and a retrieval team."

Nicole started to sob. Rick glanced at me with a look of pleading in his eyes. I took Nicole by the shoulders and held her tight. "Go ahead and do what you need to do," I said to Rick. "I'll get her back to the house. We'll wait to hear."

******

The recovery operation had been going on for what seemed like hours, and we hadn't heard anything. I understood the men wanted to retrieve whatever was there as carefully as possible so as not to disturb any evidence that might remain, but after nine months in the marsh, I had a feeling nothing would be left. On the surface, the marsh might appear to be a peaceful, even beautiful place, but I knew it was teeming with scavengers who lived and fed on anything edible. I doubted there would be anything other than bone and teeth to find.

"Did you finally get Nicole to lay down?" Brit asked after she'd helped Vikki to get Abby and the kids settled for the night.

I nodded. "She's in the den. I don't think she's asleep, but she needed some quiet time to herself. I wish they would finish the retrieval and put her out of her misery. I can't imagine how hard the not knowing must be."

"I suppose there could be another body in the marsh. It's pretty murky and dangerous," Brit pointed out.

"Possible but doubtful. The part of the marsh where the dogs reacted is protected by the dunes and thick with grass. If a body was weighted, whatever remained after the scavengers finished with it could lie there under the surface indefinitely. The land is part of the resort, so it isn't disturbed much."

"So the SOB who killed all those women killed Emily, weighed her down, and sank her in the marsh? Why?"

The bodies of the other women the FBI assumed had been strangled by Wayne Dillard were all left where they were killed. It did seem out of character for him to go to so much trouble to hide Emily's body in the marsh. The resort had been boarded up and deserted at the time he and Emily stayed here. If after months of traveling with Emily, Dillard had decided to kill her, why wouldn't he simply leave her laying on the bed as he had his other victims?"

"That's a really good question," I said at last. "Serial killers don't usually vary from their pattern."

"I suppose the deviation could have to do with Emily never fitting the pattern in the first place," Brit said. "The other victims were women in their twenties who worked in the sex industry. They were all blond and were all killed in dingy motel rooms. Emily was younger, with dark hair. She'd been with him for weeks. He knew her. Might even have liked her. Maybe she found out what he'd been doing and killed her to keep her quiet. Emily's death didn't fit the pattern, so maybe he didn't feel the need to leave things the way he normally did."

Brit had a point. If the madman Emily had been traveling with had killed her and dumped her body in the marsh, we'd find at least some of the answers we'd need to bring closure to this nightmare.

"Someone just drove up," Nicole said as she emerged from the den.

I watched out of the window as a white van with the logo of the county medical examiner pulled into the drive and was met by one of the uniformed deputies and escorted to the beach. My guess was that they were going to avoid the cabins and circle around along the beach route to the marsh.

"I guess it won't be long now," I whispered.

Brit wrapped Nicole in a huge hug as the three of us planted ourselves near the window that looked out to the marsh. We couldn't see anything because the action was too far away, but we could make out the light provided by multiple spotlights and we could hear shouting as the men communicated among themselves. Thirty minutes after the white van arrived, it left. Twenty minutes after that, Rick walked into the house through the kitchen door.

I took one of Nicole's hands in mine while Brit clung to the other.

"Well?" I asked.

"There was a body in the marsh. At this point it's little more than a skeleton."

"Emily?" Nicole whispered.

Rick shook his head. "The body had been picked at by the insects and scavengers that live in the marsh. Even the clothing was gone. But the medical examiner was able to determine it belonged to a male in his mid-to-late thirties."

"Male?" I asked.

Rick nodded.

"Who?" I said.

"We don't know. So little is left of the guy except for bones and teeth, it's going to be hard to make an ID unless we can find dental records to match up. There was a bit of soft tissue left beneath the boulder used to weigh down the body. The ME took a sample. I'm not sure he'll be able to do much with it, but again, he may be able to get some DNA. We'll have to wait and see."

"How long has he been there?" I asked. I'd stopped to enjoy the sunset from the very spot where the body had been found on many occasions. Now, it creeped me out to know there'd been a body beneath the surface all this time.

"I don't know. I suppose the ME will come up with an estimate once he's had some time with the remains. In the meantime, I'm going to take another look at missing persons reports to see if I can figure out who the victim might have been."

"So, we're back to square one in our search for Emily," Brit said.

"I'm afraid so. It's unlikely the body in the marsh has anything to do with Emily or the man she was traveling with."

Chapter 13

Tuesday, February 13

It had been a week since the body in the marsh had been retrieved. The ME still hadn't been able to make an ID and the feds were no closer to finding Emily or Dillard than ever. Tomorrow was Valentine's Day, and Jack and I had decided that despite everything, we were going to plan a romantic evening, plush with extravagant indulgence. But first, I had Abby's baby shower to cohost. Brooke Johnson had volunteered to have it in her home, so all I needed to do was bring the prizes for the games and a few party favors.

"It looks like half the women on the island are here," I commented to Brooke.

Brooke, who was married to a successful real estate professional and had a huge house, smiled. "I wanted Abby to have everything she could possibly need or even want for the baby, and this seemed like the best way to accomplish that. Besides, I love an excuse to throw a party."

I glanced at Abby, who was sitting on the sofa between Vikki and Brit, opening presents. Brit was handing her each gift to unwrap, while Vikki was jotting down notes so she'd have a record of who had given her what. Abby had started off the evening a bit shy with all the attention, but as I looked at her beaming face now, I could see she was in her element.

"I wonder where Gertie is," Brooke said. "She said she might be a few minutes late when I spoke to her earlier, but the party is half over and she still hasn't shown."

"Maybe she had a late customer or unscheduled delivery," I offered. "I'll call her."

I tried her home phone, but it just rang and rang. The woman really needed to get herself an answering machine. I'd asked her about it once before, and she'd informed me that Mortie, the ghost who lived in her house, had been freaked out by the machine when she decided to step into the current century and acquire one, so she'd gotten rid of it and never replaced it.

When I couldn't reach her at home, I tried the restaurant. She still didn't answer, but this time there was a message on the machine. I began to speak. "Hi, Gertie, it's Jill. I'm at Brooke's for the baby shower. We were wondering if you were going to make it. It's almost time for cake," I said encouragingly. I was about to hang up when Gertie came on the line.

"I'm here," Gertie said. "Something has come up. I need you to come to the restaurant."

"Are you okay?"

"I'm fine. I'll explain when you get here. Come alone."

With that, Gertie hung up.

I stared at the phone in my hand as a feeling of dread steeped into my veins.

"Is everything okay?" Brooke asked.

I slipped the phone into my pocket and forced a smile. "I'm fine. It's Gertie. Car trouble. I told her I'd go over to her place to see if I can help."

"My husband is upstairs. He's good with cars. I can send him if you'd like."

I felt a blush crawl up my cheeks. "Actually, Gertie's car is fine. I'm not sure what she wants, but she's at the restaurant and asked me to come. Alone. I made up the car thing so I'd have an excuse to sneak out."

Brooke furrowed her brows. "Do you think she's okay?"

"I'm not sure," I answered honestly. "She sounded odd. Not at all like herself."

"Maybe it's not a good idea to go alone. There's no telling what you might be walking into."

"How about if I go and check it out and text you when I get there to let you know if everything's okay? If I don't text you in, say, fifteen minutes, assume something is wrong and send reinforcements. Rick and Jack are both at the resort helping Garrett and Alex babysit Abby's kids. If I don't text you as promised, call them and tell Rick to come to Gertie's."

"Maybe you should just send Rick now and wait here where it's safe."

I shook my head. "No. Gertie did sound odd, but it could be nothing. Maybe she just had an argument with Quinten and needs to talk things through, or maybe Mortie has been kicking up his heels again and causing trouble. I don't want to overreact, but I think it's good we have a backup plan."

"Okay. I'll do as you suggest. I'll use the car excuse to explain to the others why you've left. Be careful."

"I will. Hopefully, it's nothing." Even as I said it, I knew in my gut that something awaited me.

******

When I arrived at Gertie's, the lights were on in the restaurant, and although the Closed sign was up, the front door was unlocked. I let myself in to find Gertie sitting in one of the booths across from a woman with short blond hair. I was about to introduce myself when I looked into the woman's eyes. "Emily?"

She looked down at her hands.

"Yes, this is Emily." Gertie patted the spot on the booth seat next to her. "Have a seat. Emily and I have a story to tell."

I tried to meet Gertie's eyes but, like Emily, she glanced away. I texted Brooke to let her know everything was okay, then slipped into the booth and waited for someone to fill me in.

"It's okay, sweetie," Gertie encouraged. "This is Jill. The woman I told you about. You can trust her."

I could feel my brow furrowing as I tried to figure out what in the heck was going on, but my instinct told me to wait quietly. After a minute, Emily looked up. She met my gaze.

"The body in the marsh is Wayne Dillard. I put him there nine months ago."

I wasn't expecting that, although the fact that the woman killer was dead made me happy rather than sad. "You killed him?" I asked.

"No. Not exactly." Emily's voice caught. I could see this was hard for her, so I turned and glanced at Gertie. I still wasn't sure exactly why I was here or what role Gertie intended me to play, but I had the sense that the way I responded was going to be key to getting to the bottom of whatever was going on.

"It's okay," Gertie said, patting Emily's hand. "Just start at the beginning and work up to things."

Emily nodded. She began to fold and unfold a napkin she had taken from the pile on the table. I waited quietly, content to let Emily set the pace. It was obvious she was nervous. In her place, I supposed I'd be nervous too.

She glanced out the window, then back to me, then down at the table. She seemed to be trying to work up the courage to begin. "I guess you already figured out most of it, but Gertie thinks I should tell you the whole story from my perspective," Emily said in a voice so soft I could barely make out what she was saying.

"Okay." I smiled encouragingly.

Emily's eyes darted to Gertie and then back to me. She cleared her throat and began speaking in a strong, clear voice. "Nicole Carrington is my half sister. We share a mother, although we didn't see each other very much as children. My father isn't a kind man. He beat me over every little sin he claimed I'd committed from the time I was a young child." Emily closed her eyes and took a breath, then opened her eyes and continued. "As I got older, the sins that seemed to plague me became more serious, in his eyes at least, so the beatings became both more violent and more frequent. I finally decided I'd had enough, so I made plans to run away. I knew living on the street would be hard, but nothing could be as bad as living with a man who thought I was nothing more than demon spawn."

Emily glanced down at her hands once again. Her voice softened just a bit. "In the weeks before I decided to leave my crazy father behind, I'd met a guy named Slayer. He was nice and cute, and I really liked him. He was struggling with some life issues as well, and as we got to know each other, we began to talk about taking off and seeing another part of the country. In March of last year, Slayer had a falling out with a member of the band he played with and quit to go solo. He told me he was splitting, so I decided to go with him. I'm still not sure why I called Nicole before I left, but I did. I guess I just wanted someone to know what I was doing."

Emily took a sip of her water. I didn't speak. I knew where the story was going, but I was pretty sure it would help her to tell it.

"Nicole didn't think it was a good idea for me to take off on my own. She said she was scared for me, but I knew I could take care of myself. I was afraid she'd call the cops and report me as missing, but I explained what I'd been going through at home and we worked out a deal. Part of it was that I'd send her a photo of myself every Monday so she'd know I was okay. It seemed like a good idea, and I liked having a link with someone I shared blood with."

Emily hesitated. I smiled at her, encouraging her to continue.

"After we left Bangor, Slayer told me that we were going north. When we'd talked about taking off together, we'd always talked about heading to sunny Florida, not some hick town that was even colder and more remote than the place we'd just left, but he had business up on the border."

"So you were angry?" I asked.

"Heck yeah. I'd been dreaming about the warm, sunny beach for weeks. When Slayer told me about the change of plans, I thought about ditching him and heading out on my own, but I didn't have any money or a way to get a job and support myself because I was a minor without ID. I thought about it a bit, and decided I'd just tag along with Slayer, and once we got to the hick town, I'd convince him to take me to Florida as we'd planned."

Emily paused to take another drink of water.

"After we got there, Slayer stashed me in a dumpy motel and said he was taking care of his business. I hoped it would only take a few hours, but by the second day in the frozen tundra I was done. Slayer and I had a huge fight and I took off. Somehow, I ended up at the border. While I was there, I met this man. He was an older guy, but he seemed nice, and he was heading south. He said he was fine with me tagging along, so I took the selfie I promised Nicole, then I climbed in Wayne's truck and said a mental good-bye to Slayer and the godforsaken town he'd brought me to."

"But you didn't send the photo right away," I pointed out.

"No. The plan was, I'd send a photo every Monday. It wasn't Monday yet, so I hung on to it and sent it when it was time."

"And then what?" I asked.

"And then Wayne and I headed south. It wasn't too bad at first. Like Slayer, Wayne seemed to have business to take care of. We'd drive for a while and then he'd drop me in some dive motel while he took off to take care of whatever it was he was doing." Emily's face paled. "I didn't know it at the time, but I guess he must have been busy killing those girls when he was away."

"He never gave you any indication of where he was going or what he was doing?" I asked.

Emily shook her head. "Not really, and I didn't ask. I guess I knew somehow that not asking was part of our deal. It wasn't too bad at first. Wayne would give me a few bucks and tell me he'd be back in a couple of days. He'd take off and I'd go sightseeing. After a few days, he'd come back and we'd hit the road again."

"Did he ever spend time with you other than when you were driving?"

"Sometimes he'd wait a day or two before he'd leave to take care of his business, but usually as soon as we got someplace, he'd drop me off and go. I didn't mind that he left. He had a temper. He wasn't as bad as my dad, but sometimes he'd pull my hair or slap me for no good reason."

I glanced at Gertie. I could see the rage on her face. "Did you consider leaving him while he was away?" I asked.

Emily lifted a shoulder. "A time or two, but where was I going to go? Wayne gave me money to buy food when he was gone, but not enough to support myself for long. He had a temper, but mainly my life was better with him. And when he was in a good mood, we'd have some fun. It was an okay arrangement, at least at first."

"At first?" I asked.

Emily picked up another napkin and began folding it as she had the others. "The farther south we got, the happier I was because it was warmer, but it wasn't the same for Wayne. He became agitated, and the random slaps he'd direct at me got closer together. When we got to Gull Island and he dumped me in the cabin at the closed-up resort, I was happy to be on my own for a while. It was real pretty here and so quiet. I had time to think about things, and I realized how tired I was. I started to consider leaving Wayne, but the one other time I'd made a comment about leaving, he whooped me good and hard. I knew I had to have a plan if I was going to leave him, so I decided to look for a way to make a few bucks while Wayne was away. Then I met Gertie."

Emily smiled softly at Gertie. I noticed a random tear slide down Gertie's cheek.

"Gertie was real nice to me. Nicer than anyone in my whole life. She gave me a job and some clothes. She gave me hope. When Gertie offered to let me stay and to help me find a place of my own, I wanted that very much. I felt like I'd finally found a home. I knew Wayne wouldn't want to let me go, but I had a plan to sneak away. I was thinking about that plan when I saw the news report on the television."

"At Yvette's house?"

Emily nodded. "She'd given me some clothes and had gone to get a bag to put them in. The television was on, and I saw a man talking about a woman who'd been strangled just outside Fort Collins. He had a sketch of the man who'd rented the room, and I knew right away it was Wayne. I guess I should have gone to the cops or something, but my only thought was to run. I went back to the cabin to get my stuff before Wayne came back, but he was already there. When I saw him, I ran. He must have known I'd figured out what he'd done because he chased me. He tackled me to the ground near the marsh. The next thing I knew, he had me on my back and his hands were around my throat. I knew he was going to strangle me like he did the woman in Fort Collins. I tried to fight him, but he was too strong. Just as I was about to pass out from lack of air, this giant bird flew up and landed on Wayne's head."

"Save the girl," I whispered. "It was Blackbeard letting me know he saved the girl."

"Blackbeard?" Emily asked.

"The bird that saved you. I'll explain later. Go on with your story."

Emily looked at me doubtfully but continued. "Anyway, as I was saying, this huge bird landed on Wayne's head. He jumped up and started screaming. That gave me a chance to breath. After taking a few deep breaths, I was even able to sit up. I looked toward the marsh and this bird was attacking Wayne. Wayne was waving his arms and screaming at the top of his lungs, but the bird kept flapping his wings and dive-bombing his head. Wayne was backing away from the attack, and the next thing I knew, he tripped over something and fell over backward. When he fell, he hit the back of his head on this huge boulder at the water's edge. I jumped up real quick and was going to run for my life when I saw he wasn't moving. The bird landed on a tree branch and just watched. I didn't approach him for a good long time. I was afraid it was a trick and Wayne would grab me if I got too close. Finally, I walked slowly to him. There was so much blood and his eyes were wide open but staring at nothing. I knew he was dead."

I took Emily's hand in mine. "I need you to tell me what happened next."

"I'll get in trouble."

"You won't," I assured her. "Just take your time and tell me what you remember."

Emily's lips trembled. "I remember I was scared. Real scared. But I was happy too. If that crazy bird hadn't come along, I would have been the one who was dead. I knew I should call the police, but I was a runaway who was alone with a dead man who was wanted for murder. I'd been traveling with him for over a month of my own free will. I was afraid the police would think I knew what he'd done and had kept it quiet on purpose. I was afraid the police would think I'd killed Wayne. He was laying there half in the water and half on land. I got the idea to tie a big rock to him and push him into the water the rest of the way. I knew Wayne had rope with his stuff, so I went back to the cabin and got some, then I found a big rock. It took a long time and it was hard, but eventually I managed to slip the rope under the rock, then roll Wayne over on top of it. I tied the rock to him, and then I used a tree branch for leverage and rolled him out into the marsh deep enough so he wouldn't pop up. After that I got my stuff and left."

"And since then?" I asked.

Emily looked at Gertie, who smiled with encouragement.

"I've been moving around. Working odd jobs. Getting by. I spent most of my time in Florida and was thinking about heading west when I saw a photo of myself on TV. I knew the police were looking for me, so I decided to turn myself in. I'm tired of running. I just want this whole thing to be over with."

"It will be, honey." Gertie patted the girl's hand. "It will be."

I left Gertie to fuss over Emily while I stepped outside to call Rick. I briefly explained what to expect and asked that he speak to Nicole first before bringing in the feds. When they showed up fifteen minutes later, the sisters clung to each other like they might never let go, and I knew everything was going to be okay.

Chapter 14

Wednesday, February 28

Jack and I never did get our romantic Valentine's Day dinner.

When Rick arrived, he'd had Emily go through everything again, step by agonizing step. He asked a lot of questions, so it was late into the evening before he finally called the federal agents. I had to hand it to Rick; he'd promised Emily he'd stick to her side through the entire process, and he had. The poor thing had been questioned for hours more before she was finally released into Nicole's custody, with strict instructions not to leave the resort until everything was straightened out. In the end, it was decided that, given the unique set of circumstances, Emily wouldn't be charged with any wrongdoing. She was still a minor, but she didn't want to return to her parents, so Nicole became her legal guardian until she turned eighteen. The sisters decided a change of scenery might be just the thing, so Nicole put her belongings into storage and they took off for California, where Vikki arranged for them to housesit for one of her ex-lovers while he was in Europe. It was a perfect solution that gave them the time they needed to work out their next move.

"This is really nice," I said to Jack as I sat across from him at the nicest restaurant the islands had to offer.

"I'm sorry it's fourteen days late."

I smiled and shrugged. "What's fourteen days in the grand scheme of things? I'm just happy that what looked a lot like a tragedy turned out to have a happy ending."

Jack tilted his champagne flute toward mine. "You're a sucker for a happy ending."

I took a sip of my champagne, then set my glass on the table and placed the hand I'd just freed over Jack's. "Vikki and Brit are holding down the fort at the retreat, so I'm free the whole night. What do you say we try for our own happy ending after we finish this fabulous meal?"

Jack lifted my hand and kissed the palm. "Now I know you're a mind reader because that's exactly what I was thinking."

I was about to make a comment about having slipped into the corniest of corny dialogue when my phone beeped to let me know I had a text. I wanted to ignore it, but Abby hadn't been feeling well today, so it would be careless to ignore a message from Vikki. She and Brit were on their way to the hospital with Abby while Garrett, Clara, and George kept an eye on the kids.

"Is there a problem?" Jack asked.

I looked him in the eye with longing and regret. "It's Abby. Her water broke. Brit and Vikki are taking her to the hospital."

Jack closed his menu. "I'll get the check for the champagne."

"I'm sorry. The restaurant is wonderful and I'm starving, but—"

"But you should be there. We both should. It may be a long night. We'll swing through a drive-through and grab some burgers on the way."

By the time we arrived at the hospital, Abby was in a labor room and Vikki and Brit were with her to help with the breathing exercises and to keep her mind off the contractions, which were coming quickly now. I sat in the waiting room next to Jack eating a cold hamburger wearing a dress that cost more than my first car. Jack, in his suit, had opted for chicken fingers dipped in ketchup, so I guess I shouldn't have been surprised when Brooke's mouth fell open as she skidded in through the door.

"I didn't realize this was a formal labor party." She giggled.

"French fries?" I offered her the box.

"Thanks, I've eaten. I assume you were out when you got the call?"

"You know what they say." Jack shrugged. "If you don't know what to expect, it's better to be overdressed than underdressed. This is, after all, my first labor vigil; I wasn't sure about the protocol."

"Mine too." I smiled as Brooke began to giggle even harder.

"How is she?" she asked.

"She's hanging in there," I answered. "Vikki and Brit are with her. I know first labors can take quite a while, but I think the universe owes Abby a quick and relatively pain-free delivery, so I'm hoping for the best."

"Me too." Brooke looked toward the nurses' station. "Oh, I know her. I'm going to see what I can find out."

She took off, and it was just Jack and me once again.

I tossed my half-eaten burger into the empty bag, then leaned my head against Jack's shoulder. "Can you believe that by the time we go home tonight there's going to be another person in the world? It almost seems surreal."

Jack laced his fingers through mine. "It is pretty amazing if you stop to think about it."

"If it were me about to bring a helpless baby into the world, I'd be terrified, but Abby looked pretty confident."

"She's been through a lot," Jack pointed out. "After the death of her sister, being named guardian for her nieces and nephews, and then the death of her husband, the birth of a baby is probably just a walk in the park. Besides, Abby is a strong woman. Life has tried to beat her down, but she's fought back and come out the victor. I think she's going to be just fine."

I smiled tiredly. "Yeah, me too. I just hope that if I ever bring a life into the world, I can face it with the same courage she has."

Jack turned slightly and looked at me. "Have you thought about that? Being a mom? Giving birth to an infant who shares your genes?"

I paused. "Honestly, not really. I guess I've been too busy to this point to really consider it. But I'm thirty-eight. There are a lot of people who'd consider me too old to have a first child. I don't know that I feel too old, but I guess if having a baby is something I even want to consider, I should be thinking about it now." I looked at Jack. "How about you? At forty-two, do you consider yourself too old to be a father?"

Jack's gaze narrowed. "I don't know. I don't feel old either, but even if I had a child today, I'd be sixty-five by the time he or she graduated college. There are a lot of people who have babies later in life who seem to be perfectly happy. Maybe even happier than the ones who have babies when they're too young to know what they're getting in to." Jack turned and looked directly at me. "It's odd to be having this discussion with you in a maternity ward waiting room, but it's a conversation that should be had at some point. To be honest, until now, I've never given serious thought to the matter one way or the other. I guess I figured taking the time to analyze the whole parenting thing was something I'd do later, after…"

"After what?" I asked.

"After I finished college, or finished traveling, or finished building my career, or finished whatever my goal of the moment might have been. I never felt like I was running out of time to consider the matter, but now that we're talking about it, I can see that maybe the time has come to figure it out." Jack leaned forward and kissed me on the forehead. "We should both give it some thought."

"And what if we do that? What if we give it some thought and one of us decides they want children and the other decides they don't? Then what?"

Jack tucked a lock of hair behind my ear. "I don't know how this will all work out, but I do know I love you. I never thought I'd love anyone again, but then there you were, stumbling into my life, refusing to date me unless I changed my name. I know we won't always agree on everything, and it's possible during the course of our relationship we'll hurt and then forgive each other, and we'll both be asked to make compromises. But I know that no matter what else happens, having you in my life to agree or disagree with, hurt or forgive, love and grow old with, is the most important thing. And if you consider the specifics, you'll see that in the end, nothing else really matters."

I wanted to say something memorable and heartwarming, but Brooke ran into the waiting room before I could reply. "She's here. Tammy is here. She's absolutely perfect, and Mom and baby are doing fine. Come with me." She held out a hand. "I've arranged for you to get a peek at the newest citizen of Gull Island."

NEXT FROM KATHI DALEY BOOKS

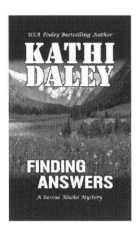

Monday, June 18

He watched the boy skipping rocks across the clear, still water. From the cover of dense forest, he listened to the childish squeals of delight as the flat, hard surface of the stone met the firm, unyielding force of the lake. Each hop resulted in an ever-widening web of rings, each ring larger yet less intense than the one that came before. Life, he mused, was like those rings. The farther you traveled from the point of origin, the wider your reach, but the less intense the effect. He'd spent a lifetime struggling to affect change in the larger rings, but now, he'd decided, it was time to avenge the iniquities of his past, to claim the inner ring as his own.

Vinnie Truman had been missing for just over an hour. The four-year-old with the sandy blond hair, big green eyes, and a smattering of freckles had been playing with his eight-year-old brother, Kip and six-year-old sister, Cammie in the yard of the cabin his parents, Jim and Joan, had rented for their summer vacation. No one saw Vinnie wander away. No one could explain why he would have.

Both Jim and Joan swore they'd been keeping an eye on their children as they grilled burgers on the deck just off the kitchen. When we walked in, Joan had been telling Officer Houston that she'd only looked away for a minute and had no idea how Vinnie could simply have disappeared.

"She's lying," I whispered to my partner, Jake Cartwright, the Rescue Alaska Search and Rescue captain.

"Why do you say that?" Jake asked, his eyes narrowing as he scanned the room, seemingly taking in the climate around us.

I looked toward the short blond woman who was wringing her hands in distress as she clung to the sturdy arm of the uniformed officer she was speaking to. "Her blouse is buttoned wrong, her feet are bare, and her hair is mussed. There may have been grilling going on, but it wasn't in the kitchen, and they weren't focused on their children."

Jake snorted, I was sure, in an effort to suppress a chuckle. "Play nice," he whispered as he stepped forward to greet the officer in charge.

"You got here fast," Hank Houston, a tall broad-shouldered man with chiseled features, dark hair, dark eyes, and a serious way about him, commented as he reached out to Jake.

"We were in the area," Jake responded as he shook the man's hand.

"This is Jim and Joan Truman," Houston introduced the obviously distressed couple. "And this is Jake Cartwright from Rescue Alaska."

"Don't worry. We're going to do everything we can to find your boy," Jake said, his voice gentle. He turned and looked at me and the two dogs with us. "This is my teammate, Harmony Carson, and our canine helpers, Sitka and Yukon."

"Officer Houston said he called for the search-and-rescue *team*," Joan said through her tears. "There are only two of you." I could see the woman was on the verge of hysteria, which could only serve to make the situation worse. "He's just a little boy. He could be injured and is probably scared. Two just won't do."

"There are a half dozen police officers looking for your boy," Houston assured her. "The search-and-rescue squad are well trained and familiar with the area. They can cover a lot of ground with just a few people and are here to lend a hand. I can assure you, ma'am, we're doing everything we can to find Vinnie."

Jake turned and looked at Joan. I watched the hard lines of his face soften as he took her hand in his. He'd been doing this a long time. He knew what to do: offer hope but get what you needed. "Harmony and I were running training exercises in the area when the call came in, so we came straight over, but we have four other highly trained members of our team in transit. We'll do everything in our power to find your boy."

Joan's face softened slightly as I imagined her clinging to that promise. I watched as she smiled slightly at Jake and then looked doubtfully toward the dogs. "Can they find him? That one looks so young."

Jake's hand visibly tightened on Joan's. "Yukon is still a puppy, but he's been doing very well with his training, and Sitka is a veteran search-and-rescue dog. He has dozens of rescues under his belt. He's one of the best at what he does, and I know he'll do his very best to find your boy. We're going to need your help, however. The most important thing you can do now is to stay strong. Can you do that? "

The woman nodded.

"Okay, good." Jake shot her a look of approval. That seemed to calm her somewhat. "First, I'll need a recent photo of Vinnie."

The man Houston had introduced as Vinnie's father handed Jake a photo he'd been holding since we'd arrived. Jake looked at it, then handed it to me. I tried to ignore the noise in the room and focus on the curious eyes and crooked grin of the boy we'd been tasked to find.

"I'll need a couple of pieces of clothing Vinnie's worn," Jake added. "The more recently they were worn, the better. Perhaps his pajamas."

"I'll get them," Vinnie's dad said, seeming grateful for something to do.

Jake nodded him, then turned his attention back to Vinnie's mother. "How long have you been staying at this cabin?"

"Almost a week." She ran a hand over her face.

"And I understand Vinnie has been missing about an hour?" Jake continued.

Vinnie's mother nodded. "Yes. We tried looking for him ourselves for a while before we called the police."

Jake continued. "Is there anywhere you've walked to in the past week that seemed to fascinate Vinnie? Anywhere he might want to return to?"

Vinnie's mother shook her head. "No. He was supposed to stay in the yard. I only looked away for a minute."

Jake looked at me. "Are you picking up anything?"

I shook my head. "Not yet." Jake didn't bother to explain to Jim and Joan that, more often than not, I was able to connect with the victims I was destined to help rescue. It certainly wasn't an exact science, and I wasn't always able to do it, but I felt as emotionally connected to the child in the photo as I felt irritated by the woman who'd been canoodling with her husband rather than watching her children.

"Where was the last place you saw your son, ma'am?" I asked as I tried to get a visual image that could help me to get a read on the boy.

"I don't know. I can't remember. It happened so suddenly." The woman was gesturing wildly with her hands, as if to make me, to make us all, understand. "One minute he was there and the next he was gone."

A fresh stream of tears started down the woman's face. "I only looked away for a minute."

"So you've said," I responded as I glanced down at the photo once again. I know it isn't my job to judge the actions of the people we're tasked to help, and I didn't have children, so I wasn't an expert when it came to the supervision of the under-ten crowd, but what I did know was that if I ever did have a child, which was highly unlikely, I wouldn't leave him or her unattended in the Alaskan wilderness.

"You'll find my boy?" Vinnie's mother pleaded after I glanced up from the photo.

"We'll try," I answered. The team I belonged to was one of the best anywhere, our survival record unmatched. Still, I'd learned at an early age that when you're battling Mother Nature, even the best teams occasionally came out on the losing end. I looked at Jake. "I'm going to head outside with the dogs. I might have better luck in a quiet environment."

After leaving the house, I sat down on a bench and instructed both dogs to sit at my feet. Sitka was an old pro at this sort of thing and waited patiently for the hunt to begin, while Yukon, sensing that something important was up, danced around on the end of his lead. I scratched him behind the ears before instructing him, again, to sit and wait. Thankfully, he did. Yukon had so much raw talent, I was certain he was going to be as good a search-and-rescue dog as Sitka eventually, but he was less than a year old and, at times, still easily distracted.

Once Yukon settled into the wait position next to Sitka, I closed my eyes and took a deep breath. I'm not sure why I'm able to connect psychically with those I'm meant to rescue. It isn't that I can feel the pain of everyone who's suffering; it seems to be only those we're meant to help that find their way onto my radar. I'm not entirely sure where the ability comes from, but I know when I acquired it. When I was seventeen, my sister Val, who was also my legal guardian after our parents' death in a car accident, went out on a rescue. She got lost in the storm, and although the team tried to find her, they came up with nothing but dead ends. I remember sitting at the command post, praying harder than I ever had. I wanted so much to have the chance to tell Val how much I loved her and, suddenly, there she was, in my head. I could feel her pain, but I also felt the prayer in her heart. I knew she was dying, but I could feel her love for me as her life slipped away. I'd tried to tell the others I knew where she was, but they'd thought my ramblings were those of an emotionally distraught teenager dealing with the fallout of shock and despair. When the team eventually found Val's body exactly where and how I'd told them they would, they began to believe I actually had made a connection with the only family I'd had left in the world.

Since then, I've used my gift to locate and rescue dozens of people. I couldn't save them all, but today, I was determined that our search for Vinnie would result in a check in the Save column. I tried to focus on the image of the child with the mischievous grin. I sensed water and was picking up the feeling of curiosity rather than fear. That was good. Chances are, as I suspected, the boy had wandered off chasing a rabbit or some other small creature and hadn't even realized he was lost yet. It was a warm day, and Vinnie's mother had assured us that he wore jeans, tennis shoes, and a hooded sweatshirt, so at least we didn't have the elements to worry about, as we did with so many of the winter rescues on which we were called out on.

I heard Yukon begin to whine. I opened my eyes and saw team members Wyatt Forrester, Dani Matthews, Landon Stanford, and Austin Brown walking toward us. Yukon stood up, preparing to greet some of his favorite people.

"Sit and wait," I reminded the pup.

He plopped his butt on the ground but continued to wag his tail. Beside him, Sitka thumped his tail without having moved an inch.

The group stopped several feet short of the dogs. The animals were working, so playful scratches and enthusiastic kisses would have to wait.

"Any news?" Dani asked.

"Jake is inside, talking to the parents. I'm sure he'll be out soon. I haven't been able to establish a clear connection to the boy, but I sense water near his current location. I don't think he realizes he's lost. I sense curiosity but not fear."

Wyatt was about to say something when Jake walked out of the house with two plastic bags, each containing a piece of clothing Vinnie had worn.

"Anything?" Jake asked me.

I told him what I'd just told the others.

"There are two bodies of water nearby," Jake said. "Eagle Lake is about a half mile up the mountain and Glacier Lake is about a half mile down the mountain from here." Jake looked around, as if sizing up the situation. "The family has hiked in both directions within the past twenty-four hours. It's likely the dogs will pick up the boy's scent in either direction, at least initially. We'll divide into two groups. I'll take Sitka,

Dani, and Austin and head up the mountain. Harmony and Yukon can work with Wyatt and Landon and head toward the lower lake." Jake looked at me. "If Yukon picks up a strong scent, radio and we can discuss a strategy. If you make a stronger connection to Vinnie, or are able to pick up anything more specific, let us know."

Jake, as Sitka's handler, and me, as Yukon's, each took a plastic bag. Once we'd cleared the yard, we let our dogs sniff the piece of clothing, telling them repeatedly, "This is Vinnie; find Vinnie." When the dogs seemed to understand what it was we were asking, we took them off their leads, then followed. I trailed directly behind Yukon, while Wyatt walked parallel to my route to the right and Landon paralleled to the left.

Once Sitka had a scent, he was usually very focused on the task at hand, so the odds of Jake and his team finding Vinnie if he had traveled up the mountain were great. Yukon, on the other hand, was pretty green. He had been abandoned on my doorstep five months earlier, and I, as I always did, had taken him in. Over the course of the next month, I'd worked to teach him the house rules. During the course of his training, I'd noticed what I felt was an innate ability to find whatever it was I sent him to look for. I spoke to Jake, and he agreed to help me train him for search and rescue. We'd discussed needing a second dog. Yukon caught on to the training like a fish to water, and although he'd only been training for a few months, he'd already been successful in locating the victim in five different simulations. Of course, a real rescue was a lot more intense than a simulation for both dog and handler, and this was the first time he'd participated in a real rescue without Sitka by his side to show him how it was done.

Yukon headed into the dense foliage of the nearby forest and I followed. I glanced at Wyatt, who was perhaps fifty yards to my right, and then Landon, who was fifty yards to my left. They nodded, letting me know they were able to follow despite the rough terrain. I glanced at Yukon, who sniffed the air and headed deeper into the forest. While we searched, I kept an eye on him, but basically let him do his thing. After several minutes, he alerted, showing interest where a fallen tree blocked the path. "Did you find something?" Yukon sniffed the log and wagged his tail. "Good boy." I looked around and called Vinnie's name. Nothing. I stood perfectly still and closed my eyes. I waited for a vision to appear. I could sense the boy, but, as before, he didn't seem frightened. But there was something. Something dark. Something menacing. I tried to hone in on it, but I couldn't get a clear reading, so I tied a flag to a tree branch to mark the spot, then took the pajama top out of the bag. I once again held it under Yukon's nose. "This is Vinnie. Find Vinnie." Yukon set off down the trail. I went after him.

I knew once Vinnie realized he was lost, fear would overcome him. That would help me to connect with him, yet I hoped for his sake we'd find him before he became terrified. The forest was thick with evergreens and underbrush. Yukon had left the trail after we'd come across the fallen log, which meant Vinnie most likely had left the trail as well. The area was home to a variety of wildlife, including grizzlies, wolves, and cougars. It was dangerous for anyone to veer off the established trail, but it was especially dangerous for little boys who had no idea that danger lurked in the dark places beyond the clearing.

It wasn't easy to both follow Yukon and focus on Vinnie. If we didn't either hear from Jake or find him in the next few minutes, I'd call to the dog to take a break.

As we approached the lake, Yukon alerted again. As before, I stopped and looked around. I called for Vinnie and then listened. I closed my eyes and tried desperately to make a connection. This time, the vision was a bit clearer. Vinnie had stopped what he was doing to look around. He must have realized he was lost and, as predicted, curiosity had been replaced by fear.

"Harmony to Jake," I said through the radio.

"Go ahead."

"I have a vision. He's near Glacier Lake."

"We're on our way."

I closed my eyes and focused again. He was terrified. Fear and panic fueled the boy as he ran through the underbrush. I cringed as I saw him trip over something. Pain. Now the fear was mingled with pain. He got up and tried to run, but the pain was too much. When he fell again, he simply sat on the ground, clutching his ankle and screaming for help. I took a deep breath. There was something else. Darkness. Danger.

I opened my eyes and looked at Yukon. "Find Vinnie. We need to find Vinnie." I gave him another sniff of the pajama top and waited. He sniffed, the air then took off at a run. I tried unsuccessfully to keep up with him and was about to call him back when I heard three sharp barks.

"Vinnie," I called as loudly as I could.

"Here. I'm here."

I headed down the trail as quickly as I could manage. Sprawled on the ground was a terrified little boy with his arms around Yukon, who gently licked the tears from his face.

"Good boy," I said to Yukon. I knelt down next to Vinnie. "Are you hurt?"

"My ankle. I hurt my ankle."

I radioed Jake to let him know I'd found Vinnie. He would need to be carried back to the cabin, so I waited for Wyatt and Landon to catch up.

"Other than your ankle, do you hurt anywhere?" I asked.

The boy shook his head. He was smiling now that Yukon had settled in next to him. "I was lost. I was on the trail, but then I looked around and nothing looked right. I was so scared. I ran as fast as I could. I wanted to get home, but then I fell."

I looked back the way Vinnie had traveled. "Did you trip on a log?"

Vinny wiped the tears from his dirt-streaked face. "I don't know. I didn't see."

I radioed Jake and the others, then brought my focus back to Vinnie. "Help is on the way. We'll get you home in no time. You're safe now."

"Mama will be mad. I'm not supposed to leave the yard." The boy began to sob. "I'm going to get a time-out. I hate time-outs."

I pulled my sweatshirt over my head and used it to wipe away the boy's tears. "I can't say for certain, but I think your mom will be so happy to see you that she might forget to be mad. Still, the rule about staying in the yard is a good one. You could have been in real trouble if Yukon didn't find you. There are all sorts of things out here that can hurt a little boy."

"Like bears?"

I nodded. "Yes, like bears. And cougars, and wolves, and all sorts of animals that might be lurking nearby, waiting to attack."

The boy began to sob hysterically. Yukon began to lick his face frantically to offer comfort. Okay, so maybe I oversold the danger angle. I didn't mean to traumatize the kid; I just wanted him to understand the potential consequences of his actions.

"What's wrong?" Wyatt said, arriving in the nick of time as far as I was concerned. He bent down and picked the boy up in his arms. "Are you hurt?"

"No." The boy began to hiccup as a result of his hysteria.

"So why all the tears?"

"I was bad and a bear might have ate me."

Wyatt looked at me and raised a brow.

I lifted a shoulder. "It's not like I have experience talking to kids. Dogs are more my thing."

Wyatt winked at me. "You did good. Yukon too. Let's get this scared little boy back to his parents."

"Wait," I said as Wyatt turned to head back to the cabin. I stood up and slowly scanned the forest as Landon arrived. I could still sense the darkness I'd picked up before. I couldn't identify what I was feeling, but an iciness settled into my chest. I felt pain and hopelessness and death. "There's someone else. Someone near death." I closed my eyes and concentrated. The image of a man's face filtered through my mind, but it was blurry and out of focus. It was as if the man was passing in and out of consciousness, letting me in and then pushing me out. "Oh God," I whispered.

"What is it?" Wyatt said. "What do you see?"

I glanced at Vinnie, who looked scared to death. I tried to level my voice despite the intense grief that had gripped my body. "Go ahead and take Vinnie back to his parents. Landon, Yukon, and I will try to find the source of my vision."

Wyatt looked uncertain, but he didn't argue. He nodded and began walking back toward the cabin. When he was out of sight, I closed my eyes and tried to see the face of the man again. Landon stood quietly next to me, holding Yukon's lead. He took my hand in his free one and held on tight. He'd been with me long enough to know how draining this was for me.

"Anything?" Landon asked in a voice so soft I barely heard him.

"It isn't focused. It's a man. I can't see his face. He's hurt. His image is fading in and out. He doesn't want to let me in." My breath caught as I connected just in time to experience what I was sure was the man's last breath. I shook my head, then opened my eyes. "He's gone."

"Where?"

I looked through the dense forest. "I don't know. I wasn't linked for more than a few seconds. He was resisting, but I managed to connect right at the end, when his only choice was to surrender. Now that he's dead I can't sense him." I looked around at the thick trees. "We'll need help to find him." I radioed Jake and informed him of the situation, then Landon, Yukon, and I began to search for the man I had seen in my mind.

Jake's dog, Sitka, had been trained to find missing people as well as those who had already passed on. Yukon was training to follow a specific scent, as we'd just done with Vinnie, but he had no training as a cadaver dog. Our best bet at finding the man whose death I had just experienced was to force myself to remember everything about that moment. Everything I had seen, heard, smelled, and felt.

"The man was lying on the ground," I said in a soft voice. "He was cold. Weak. Wet, perhaps. He was partially covered, but the purpose of the cover wasn't to provide warmth but camouflage."

"You said wet? Is he near the water?" Landon asked.

"Maybe. It's dark. The trees in the area are dense." I opened my eyes and scanned the area. I could remember the pain, the fear, the urge to fight, and then the peace that came with the decision to give in and float away from the world toward whatever came next.

"Are you okay?" Landon asked.

I nodded.

Landon used his thumb to wipe a tear from my cheek. "I know it's painful."

"It's okay. I'm okay," I assured him. There are times I want to run from the images and feelings that threaten to overwhelm and destroy me, but I know embracing the pain and the fear is my only path to the answers I seek. "In the last moment of his life, there was fear, anger, and pain, but something else as well." I focused harder. "Acceptance and," I tried to remember, "penance. He was sorry for something he did and with his last breath was seeking forgiveness."

"From whom?" Landon asked.

I opened my eyes. "I don't know. Maybe God. Maybe himself. Maybe someone he'd wronged." I continued to scan the forest, looking for something familiar. The only thing I could see in my vision was trees, which didn't help me a bit because there were trees everywhere.

"Do you remember anything from your vision that will help us know where to look?" Landon asked again. "Anything at all that will help us narrow things down?"

"There were trees and it was dark." I took a breath and forced my mind to calm and focus. "The ground was gently sloped and covered with wild grass." I bit my lip as I tried to get a feel for direction. "There." I pointed into the distance.

Landon set off in the direction I indicated with Yukon at his side. I followed closely behind. Shortly after we'd entered the densest part of the forest, Yukon began to whine.

"Do you have the scent?"

Yukon barked three times.

"Let him go," I instructed Landon. "He may not be trained to retrieve those who have passed on, but he's a dog and therefore better able to pick up scent than either of us."

It didn't take long. Really no longer than it took to take a breath for Yukon to find the body. I felt my knees weaken and my stomach lurch. "It's Pastor Brown." I gasped as Landon bent down and took a closer look at the man who was partially covered by the thick underbrush.

"If only we'd been a few minutes sooner," I said to Landon as he pulled away the vines and ferns that someone seemed to have arranged from the man's body. He knelt and felt for a pulse, then shook his head. The pastor's throat had been slit and he had a piece of duct tape across his mouth.

"He couldn't even scream," I said, as if that somehow made it worse.

"I wonder how he got here," Landon said.

I felt the hairs on the back of my neck stand up. Yukon began to growl from deep in his chest as I scanned our surroundings. I didn't see or hear anything, but my intuition told me that Pastor Brown's killer was still nearby. "Someone brought him here. Someone who's still here."

Landon stood up and looked around. "I don't see anything. Are you sure you sense a second person?"

"I'm not a hundred percent sure, but I do sense someone. I don't feel as if he's a threat to us, though. I'll call Jake to have him fill Officer Houston in on what we've found."

I made the call, then returned my attention to Landon, who was still standing over the body. We both knew not to touch him because we could destroy evidence, but in that moment not touching was very difficult indeed. I'd felt the man's life leave his body. There was a voice in my head that demanded I do something better than simply stand there.

"It looks like he'd been swimming," I said. He was soaking wet, but he was fully dressed, and it was much too cold to have gone swimming in a lake whose source was melting snow, so the idea was probably ridiculous.

"I doubt that, but he is wet," Landon replied. He nodded to the pastor's bloody wrists without touching him. "It looks like he was bound at some point, though there are no signs of any ropes here."

"Maybe he was tossed from a boat and swam to shore," I suggested. "Once he made it to land, the cold-blooded killer who dumped him in the water slit his throat and left him to die."

"Maybe," Landon replied. "Someone tried to camouflage the body. I'm guessing he'd passed out before he died. Maybe he *was* tossed from a boat and swam to shore before he was killed." Landon paused and turned his head. "It sounds like the others are almost here."

Books by Kathi Daley

Come for the murder, stay for the romance.

Zoe Donovan Cozy Mystery:

Halloween Hijinks
The Trouble With Turkeys
Christmas Crazy
Cupid's Curse
Big Bunny Bump-off
Beach Blanket Barbie
Maui Madness
Derby Divas
Haunted Hamlet
Turkeys, Tuxes, and Tabbies
Christmas Cozy
Alaskan Alliance
Matrimony Meltdown
Soul Surrender
Heavenly Honeymoon
Hopscotch Homicide
Ghostly Graveyard
Santa Sleuth
Shamrock Shenanigans
Kitten Kaboodle
Costume Catastrophe
Candy Cane Caper
Holiday Hangover
Easter Escapade
Camp Carter

Trick or Treason
Reindeer Roundup
Hippity Hoppity Homicide
Fireworks Fiasco – *June 2018*

Zimmerman Academy The New Normal
Ashton Falls Cozy Cookbook

Tj Jensen Paradise Lake Mysteries by Henery Press:

Pumpkins in Paradise
Snowmen in Paradise
Bikinis in Paradise
Christmas in Paradise
Puppies in Paradise
Halloween in Paradise
Treasure in Paradise
Fireworks in Paradise
Beaches in Paradise – *July 2018*

Whales and Tails Cozy Mystery:

Romeow and Juliet
The Mad Catter
Grimm's Furry Tail
Much Ado About Felines
Legend of Tabby Hollow
Cat of Christmas Past
A Tale of Two Tabbies
The Great Catsby
Count Catula
The Cat of Christmas Present
A Winter's Tail
The Taming of the Tabby

Frankencat
The Cat of Christmas Future
Farewell to Felines
The Cat of New Orleans – Part of the Spell or High
Water Anthology – *June 2018*
A whisker in Time – *July 2018*

Writers' Retreat Southern Seashore Mystery:
First Case
Second Look
Third Strike
Fourth Victim
Fifth Night
Sixth Cabin

Rescue Alaska Paranormal Mystery:
Finding Justice
Finding Answers – *May 2018*

A Tess and Tilly Mystery:
The Christmas Letter
The Valentine Mystery
The Mother's Day Mishap

Sand and Sea Hawaiian Mystery:
Murder at Dolphin Bay
Murder at Sunrise Beach
Murder at the Witching Hour
Murder at Christmas

Murder at Turtle Cove
Murder at Water's Edge
Murder at Midnight

Haunting by the Sea:
Homecoming By The Sea
Secrets By The Sea – *June 2018*

Seacliff High Mystery:
The Secret
The Curse
The Relic
The Conspiracy
The Grudge
The Shadow
The Haunting

Road to Christmas Romance:
Road to Christmas Past

USA Today best-selling author Kathi Daley lives in beautiful Lake Tahoe with her husband Ken. When she isn't writing, she likes spending time hiking the miles of desolate trails surrounding her home. She has authored more than seventy-five books in eight series, including Zoe Donovan Cozy Mysteries, Whales and Tails Island Mysteries, Sand and Sea Hawaiian Mysteries, Tj Jensen Paradise Lake Series, Writers' Retreat Southern Seashore Mysteries, Rescue Alaska Paranormal Mysteries, and Seacliff High Teen Mysteries. Find out more about her books at **www.kathidaley.com**

Stay up to date:

Newsletter, The Daley Weekly
http://eepurl.com/NRPDf
Kathi Daley Blog – publishes each Friday
http://kathidaleyblog.com
Webpage – www.kathidaley.com
Facebook at Kathi Daley Books –
www.facebook.com/kathidaleybooks
Kathi Daley Books Group Page –
https://www.facebook.com/groups/569578823146850/
E-mail – kathidaley@kathidaley.com
Twitter at Kathi Daley@kathidaley –
https://twitter.com/kathidaley
Amazon Author Page –
https://www.amazon.com/author/kathidaley
BookBub – https://www.bookbub.com/authors/kathi-daley
Pinterest – http://www.pinterest.com/kathidaley/

JUL 1 9 2018

South Lake Tahoe

75463801R00109

Made in the USA
San Bernardino, CA
01 May 2018